You think you've got troubles? Disaster lives with Neil Nudelman! He's feeding his family from the garbage bins behind the A&P. He's arrested, beaten, harassed by his neighbors, betrayed by his friends. Watching helplessly as bedlam rages and "life comes crashing down about [his] ears," Nudelman struggles for subsistence, sanity and some shred of human dignity. Sounds horrible? But it's not! In fact, Lieberman has pulled off one of the funniest and literate books of the decade, capturing the pain of America and letting you laugh at it. You'll laugh until it hurts.

GOOBERSVILLE BREAKDOWN

GOOBERSVILLE
BREAKDOWN

By

**Robert
Lieberman**

Illustrated by
Tom Parker

GAMMA BOOKS

First Printing Dec. 1978
Second Printing Jan. 1979
Third Printing Jan. 1979

Designed by Mary A. Scott
Cover illustration by Tom Parker

LIBRARY OF CONGRESS CATALOGING IN PUBLICATION DATA

Lieberman, Robert H.
  Goobersville Breakdown.

  I. Title.
PZ4.L723Go   [PS3562.I44]   813'.5'4   78-74110

Quality Paperback   ISBN 0-933124-00-7
Cloth   ISBN 0-933124-01-7

For Gunilla

"Wealth is not without its advantages and the case to the contrary, although it has often been made, has never proved widely persuasive"

John Kenneth Galbraith
The Affluent Society

Yesterday I awoke with a case of cancer. The rest of the day went as usual. By evening things were going decidedly better—I was only suffering from anxiety. The day before it was kidney failure—I could only pee a pint and was seriously considering a transplant. When will I learn to be grateful for small illnesses?

According to the latest reckoning of the labor department (Viveca and the boys), I am well into my third year of unemployment. Three years of staring out the window at the woods and watching the seasons change, with only the spasmodic relief of an occasional odd job.

In addition to being a *Luftmensch*, someone who can exist solely on air, I also hold the back-up title of being a "freelance anything"—which is pretty safe because in Goobersville, as they say, you can't find nothing . . . Funny though, in my mind's eye I still can't quite make the leap from professorial splendor to full-time poverty . . . Three years. Three years of not having income, and coming finally to resent those poor souls who do. At this instant in time I am well beyond the verge of bankruptcy. I have milked friendship to the very hilt. I slink through town hoping to avoid eyes. The bill collector would be beating at the door except that it entails a mile long march through hip deep snow and the chances are pretty slim that he'd even find our house in the woods. When I am threatened with the imminent danger of becoming a poor credit risk I laugh, whistle through my teeth, stand on my head and do a jig. What do they know of risks? From

9

respected pillar of the Goobersville community, I have tumbled down to cheating the phone company, siphoning off electricity from the power people, poaching, pilfering, bamboozling, wheeling, dealing, as well as making a thorough nuisance of myself—all to say that, even though I have fallen on hard times, I suspect I'm still alive and kicking, determined not to let the shits get me down—which, I suppose, is what *this* is all about.

But I'm getting ahead of myself again. So much to say and suddenly, I feel rushed. What a joke. I'm even laughing. After three years of nothing I feel rushed. Have to get it all down. Yes. Three years. Final warnings. Collection notices. Empty tummies. No prospects of employment. Yet I feel remarkably chipper for a man with cancer, heart condition, brain tumors and halitosis. And on top of all that I also feel guilty for feeling so good. Or do I? Such conflicts. Such insanity. When will it all end?

.   .   .

Dear Friend,

This letter may at first strike you as a form letter. Well, I suppose it is, but please be assured that I am sending it in lieu of a personal note only because of the exigencies of time.

Since my last letter the condition of our family— morally, spiritually, ethically, but worst of all financially—has rapidly deteriorated.

You have been placed on this particular mailing because in the past you have shown yourself to be a humane, concerned and charitable inhabitant of this planet—a cut above the rest. In all probability you have already been called upon and sent money to CARE and UNICEF, supported a family in Seoul, given to Biafra Relief, sent life-giving supplies to Managua and Tegucigalpa. With the

10

Heart Fund, Easter Seals, and American Cancer Society eagerly vying for your hard-earned dollars, I'm sure you are more than weary of letters soliciting further funds. But, please, before you throw away this urgent appeal, just give me a moment to point out some facts of which you may not be aware, namely, that by making a tax-deductible contribution to the SAVE THE NUDELMAN FEDERATION you will not only be helping a needy family, but *also* supporting the arts. Your dollars sent to me go twice as far as in any other charitable institution. We have absolutely no overhead, no costly outlays for office equipment or help. Our only expense is the stamp on this letter and even that has been stolen. EVERY ONE OF YOUR DOLLARS GOES DIRECTLY TO US. No middleman. No foundation officials raking off the top. Your hard-won bucks are not turned into wheat that is allowed to rot or be nibbled away by rats in a Calcutta port. Your pipe-lined dollars will be giving not only sustenance, but also moral support to a family right here in the USA, right here in good old Goobersville, N.Y.

And here's what your *tax deductible* contribution can accomplish:

$5 will provide one full nourishing meal for the entire family consisting of meat, salad, quart of milk, and modest dessert.

$10 will send one of my children off to school with a new pair of shiny shoes.

$25 will provide the children this year with either a Hanukkah or Christmas gift (please indicate preference).

$100 will stave off foreclosure on our home by one full month.

$500 will provide proof of lasting friendship, will bring tears to the eyes of this writer, and will be celebrated by your name being added to a bronze honor roll plaque erected at the top of Mt. Nudelman.

As my good friend Dr. Malvin Mandel is inclined to say, "There are some people who, by virtue of the way they live, deserve to be supported by the rest of us." I am in complete agreement with this rational philosophy and, needless to say, a copy of this letter has gone to Dr. Mandel in this mailing.

Dear friend, even though I sleep until noon, have forgotten what it's like to be gainfully employed, can not recall the feeling of punching a clock or paying Social Security, I would like to assure you that I am neither having a ball, nor will I be living it up on your sweat-earned dollars while each day you must endure the indignity of being cooped up in your office, forced to don a crisp white shirt on those icy winter mornings, or ride the B.M.T.

If it is any solace and eases the pain of parting with an infinitesimal grain of your wealth, let me tell you that up to now my life has been sheer agony. I sleep until noon each day solely out of necessity—I suspect I may be suffering from either narcolepsy, encephalitis, or both. The migraines that I used to experience bimonthly when you first got to know me, have become nearly a daily occurrence. As you may realize, worry has a way of eating up a person. A man needs small victories to wipe out the big defeats. Instead of granting me a strong back and weak mind, God has screwed things up and given me just the opposite. My kids have even had worms. What has this to do with a weak mind? Absolutely nothing, except to show you how my thoughts drift because of the constant pressure of worry—a pressure that only *you* can relieve.

Sure, for the time being it's cheaper sending money to Asia. Six dollars, which can sustain an Indonesian family for a month, would hardly feed my car. But one day, when I'm rich and famous (which is as inevitable as bread molding) I shall not forget your kindness, I shall repay every penny, I shall even adopt a Brazilian child by mail through the *Foster Parents' Plan*.

Thank you and may God grant speed to your check-filled letters.

Yours,

Neil H. Nudelman

Neil H. Nudelman
Executive Director of the
S.T.N.F.

Purely by chance I have stumbled on an ingenious route to economic survival. It is so simple that in retrospect I can't help but wonder why it took me virtually years to discover it. In its barest form, the strategy consists of just saying "No," refusing to buy anything that costs money. No to new clothes. No to new furnishings, tools or toys. No to any expenditures except vital necessities—which, having mastered the technique, cease to be vital. And saying *No,* a man leaves himself a chance to maneuver, while to say *Yes* is to make a costly commitment. It's so utterly fool-proof and clever that I am covered with goose-pimples and overcome with the irresistible desire to hug myself.

3 P.M. Leif comes running up through the woods home from Goobersville Elementary School excitedly waving a piece of paper. "I can have ski lessons!" he shouts, dropping his lunch pail on the dog who lies dozing by the door. "And they give you the skis, too. Look!" He hands me the paper that each of the third graders has gotten from the teacher.

Being an American I am vaguely skeptical. Nothing is for free except gonorrhea. I look. My suspicions are confirmed.

"And it's only thirty dollars."

I employ my new-fangled economic ploy, "No."

"Daddy, please," Leif says, hugging me around the waist. He looks up at me with those warm, long-lashed eyes and I feel myself soften. Leif has always talked about skiing.

We live in ski country. All the kids have skis. All the kids have fancy downhill skis with double boots and safety bindings, matching pants and jacket. All the kids have fathers who work.

"And they take you from school by bus to the lifts. And you *ride* up. To the top of the hill!"

"You have a sled and a whole mountain. Tell me, how many other kids have their own mountain? Huh? Stop being greedy."

I watch the boy's eyes cloud up.

"Look," I say, picking him up and holding him like the little boy that he is, "thirty dollars is a fortune. If I had it, I'd give it to you even if skiing is a bourgeois affectation, which it is."

"You used to ski," says Leif, looking for an opening.

"I used to do a lot of things," I pat his head. "Listen, times aren't good." I struggle to explain and, to my surprise Leif—a usually tenacious little boy—gives up and disappears into the basement.

"All he's talked about for the last year is skiing," Viveca explains sympathetically, rubbing in a little salt.

"I know, I know, I'm a shit. But what can I do? Say yes, here's thirty bills?"

Viveca shrugs and sighs. I want the earth to open and swallow me, but before I can berate the powers that be, there emerges from the basement a terrible din. "See," I smile relieved, pleased for once at the noise from the boys. "He's already forgotten. Kids have short memories. Christ, if you bought them everything they wanted bla bla bla." Vaguely, I am beginning to sound like an Archie Bunker to my own ears.

Curious later, I walk down the narrow stairs into the basement. There I discover Leif working away, busily nailing pieces of elastic to a length of scavenged wood molding. Little curly-headed, angelic Magnus, serious first grader that he is, is helping his big brother knock in nails at random with a hammer twice his size.

15

"Leif's making a ski," Magnus chirps.

"I'm making a *pair* of skis," explains Leif, trying to pin the flimsy rubber under a bent over nail. "Can you hammer this down?"

"Look, the elastic's too thin to hold and even if you could keep your feet on, you can't ski on flat boards. They have to be bent up in the front, otherwise they'll get stuck in the snow," I explain, feeling a wave of sadness sweep over me, his determination to have skis apparent even to a bumbling, thick-skinned fool like myself. An ingenious economic strategy? Horseshit! I am asking little kids to see reason, behave like thirty-year-old jaded adults. The thought of shoplifting crosses my mind. How do you hide a pair of skis and poles under a trench coat? I follow Leif's orders and fasten the rubber.

"No. Put it here," he insists knowingly.

"Really, I don't think it'll quite work," I try to prepare my boy for his defeat as he squirms into his snow suit torn at the sleeves, his mis-matched gloves, heelless boots. As I glance down at him it's as though I am seeing for the first time all the squalor caused by my neglect.

"Leif's gonna ski!" Magnus squeals excitedly, lying on his back, his feet in the air, patiently waiting for someone to help him on with his boots.

I follow the team of optimistic brothers as they emerge from the house and enter the woods. The trees are heavy with a fresh wet snow, the air crisp and sharp to my nostrils. Standing on the little hill in front of the house, Leif gropes to find the elastic under the snow.

"Here, let me give you a hand," I suggest, and obligingly I help stick his feet in the loose rings of rubber. "Won't hold," I try to remind as Magnus, his cherubic cheeks red with cold, peers over my shoulder, one hand gently resting on my arm.

"Hold me up," says Leif, hanging onto my sleeve, his feet now vaguely in position. "O.K. Now. Push me," he orders.

"You'll bog right down."

"Push me!"

I pick him up and get his molding boards above the level of snow and begin to move forward. To my utter amazement he is actually sliding forward, staying above the snow. I let go and he still continues to slide, his feet wobbling in the contraption, his mouth open, but picking up speed. Down. Down. Down he glides above the powder leaving a parallel trail like an Aspen pro.

"He's skiing! He's skiing!" Magnus jumps up and down.

"He's skiing!" Viveca cries, leaning out from the kitchen window in disbelief. "Look!"

I'm looking. I'm looking. The tears begin to well up in my eyes and I fight to keep from weeping. Leif crosses his skis, falls face forward and then emerges laughing.

"You see!" he shouts, jubilantly picking up his skis, the elastic torn and dangling. "It works!"

"Of course it works!" I snap, having learnt my lesson, and quickly I rush back to the house to make myself a pair of those things. Got any more elastic?

.   .   .

Leif pulled me out of bed at six a.m. this morning to ask a pressing question. He wants to know what he can invent in order to become a millionaire. He is still entranced with the American dream. The only American dream I ever had was a wet one.

I told Leif that he should try to invent some sort of ray, like a laser, that can be used to break down the molecular structure of an animate object, leaving behind only dust or maybe a little puddle.

"Who would buy it?" he asks, his dark almond eyes peering serious out from below a line of overgrown blond bangs.

"I would. I'd use it to evaporate the Szorskys, the planes that keep bugging us overhead, the . . ."

"But you don't have any money."

"Who says? Anyway I'll be rich one day. Just a matter of time."

"Why don't you get a job?"

"Stop being a *kvetch*. For a nine-year-old you sound like an old lady. Why don't you go brush your teeth. You haven't done it in a month. Your teeth are all gonna fall out."

"Good. Then I'll get a dollar from the tooth fairy for every tooth."

"Is money the *only* thing you think about?"

"Yup."

.   .   .

One Mt. Nudelman Rd.
Goobersville, N.Y.

Mr. Mao Tse Tung, Chairman
The People's Republic of China
China

Dear Mr. Tse Tung,

It has come to my attention that there may shortly be an opening in your country for a math teacher and I would like to pursue with you the possibilities of such employment.

I have a broad and very unusual background, having taught in such varied institutions as predominantly black colleges in the South, a technical lyceum in the Swedish arctic, and even a school for Chinese students in Hong Kong (though admittedly the pupils were the offspring of wealthy entrepreneurs and businessmen).

I would best fit, I think, into a small, four-year,

18

liberal arts college setting, in a position teaching Basic Calculus and Differential Equations—though I might even be willing to teach Advanced Calculus, or for that matter Physics. Come to think of it, I'd even gladly teach English or Swedish or German to your students. Perhaps I should also add parenthetically that for a while I studied veterinary medicine—so when I'm not busy in the classroom I could assist in curing some of your country's animals. Oh, I almost forgot. I've also studied a good deal of Organic and Inorganic Chemistry—so you see, Mr. Chairman, there are no limits to my skills and, to be perfectly frank, I am getting a bit desperate to find work.

Examination of my credentials may give you the false impression that I have the tendency to jump around from field to field simply because I can't hack it. Let me, however, hasten to point out that the repeated changes in my areas of specialization and sites of employment were the sole result of a *carefully* mapped out strategy, an attempt to broaden myself both as an individual and as an academician. Furthermore, I was beginning to discover that I just simply wasn't made to be a scientist confined to one field, one desk, one office. As my friend Perry-the-roofer is inclined to quote in reference to my unusual situtation, "You can't put a saddle on a chicken."

In my ten years of university and college teaching I have been known as a "dynamic teacher, exceedingly popular with his pupils." On numerous occasions I have demonstrated myself to be a high grader and, with time, have even learned to further moderate my demands upon students. I realize that I was fired from my last job, however, given an opportunity I'm sure I could explain the extenuating circumstances involved in that cruel and ill-considered separation.

I have very strong liberal credentials: I voted for

Hubert Humphrey in 1964 though not in 1968; I have marched in countless peace demonstrations; and I have been harassed and abused by the KKK while living in Virginia.

Although the free enterprise system has given me all I have today, I think you will find my politics exceedingly flexible. Communist. Capitalist. Socialist. Fascist. It's all one bowl of soup and when you're hungry (as I know you have been) well, soup is soup.

Flexibility. I have to laugh at myself. I can't help but think back to the time when I was a bright young, just-about-to-be-graduated Electrical Engineer, at the top of my class, in those bountiful years when being an Electronics Scientist was close to being a god; when companies flew me back and forth across the continent—not to interview me, but to give me a chance to interrogate their staff, see how they operate, interview *them*!

Pick and chose! That was me, a twenty-year-old, smartass, honor student with a well-greased slide rule and firm principles. To this day I can still clearly recall how, on those same principles, I refused to even contemplate working for any company vaguely connected with defense work. Principles. Today I'm slowly getting the inkling of how men can trot off so easily to war. Sometimes a man can be beaten down so low, feel so impotent and angry and apathetic in the same foul breath that all he craves is change, any kind of change—so stick a gun in my hand, point me at the target and I'm raring to go. What I'm saying, Mr. Chairman, is that politics is rapidly becoming a moot question with me as flexibility, I fear, has long since become a byword.

Maybe, as long as we're being so open, I should also confess another fear that has recently come to plague me, namely, that I'm already beginning to lose my mind, that my years of worry have finally started to take their toll. Occasionally—especially in the wee hours of the morning while the rest of the world sleeps—I find myself becoming deathly scared that if things don't improve I will shortly go mad. But please don't worry. This occurs, as I mentioned, *only* occasionally and would certainly not interfere with my daytime teaching duties. And even if I was teaching night school, things have a way of working themselves out—if you know what I mean. And somehow I get the feeling that having gone through what you have in your lifetime you *can* grasp what I'm struggling to say.

I don't really know how to put this without sounding corny, but I think, for the first time, I *really* understand what it's like to be black. Yesterday, by chance, I was looking at a picture taken at an upstate prison and as I searched the faces of the men I actually had a hard time finding a white one. Suddenly it all fell into line. They're being locked in there for the same reason I suspect I will shortly one day be locked away—to keep them, me, us, out of society. We're all niggers of a sort. Our hands are bound. Our minds are set. We can't be plugged into this culture. Like them, I am a social misfit, hopelessly out of step. And finally I'm beginning to get the message—that there is little place in this society for writers other than those who will either write commercials or be commercial.

Enclosed with this letter please find my curriculum vitae together with glowing letters of recommendation from former Deans who were relieved to get me off their hands at such a low price. I am also submitting an in-depth description of my educational philosophy and hope you won't take offense.

In closing, let me add that I am certain that my

family and I would have little trouble adapting to the ways of your country. My wife and I are exceedingly fond of Chinese food and whenever we are in New York City we always go to Chinatown for dinner—and not just because it is the cheapest place in town to eat.

Should you need more information, please feel free to call upon me. I anxiously look forward to your reply and wish to thank you in advance for your generosity.

Yours truly,

Neil H. Nudelman

Neil H. Nudelman

P.S. If worse comes to worse I could also write propaganda, provided of course that it is not of a commercial nature.

This morning, while checking out a job opening that turns out not to exist, I bump into my old friend Perry-the-roofer. Well, not exactly bump into him. Walking aimlessly through the downtown I hear a distant voice calling me and, after looking all around, I finally stare up to discover him waving to me from high atop the Court House roof. In his own laconic way he's been up there every day for the last two weeks, it seems, monitoring the comings and goings of Goobersville.

"Seen you scurrying around down there looking for a job," he explains after I climb a series of wobbly ladders and clatter across the steep, icy roof, reaching the stretch he has shoveled clear of snow. From where he sits, I note, you can actually observe the whole city, so there's no sense denying the truth.

"Well, I've been sort of looking around a little," I smile embarrassed. "What else have you seen?"

"Seen you sneaking the old popcorn from behind the Goobersville Theater," says Perry his long, sharp face breaking into a smile as he bites his cigarette.

"That was to feed the birds," I lie.

"Popcorn?" he lifts his eyebrows knowingly.

"What are you doing up here on a roof in the middle of winter?"

"What's it look like?" he laughs and sets me to work tossing him shingles from a platform that sits nailed to the roof.

I feed him a stack, then climb back up and sit straddling the peak of the Court House roof. Relaxing and staring out over the snowy rooftops of the entire city, I begin to understand Perry's fascination with roofing. Since coming back from Vietnam, Perry has been progressively pulling away from mankind. And what better profession could he choose, I think leaning against a chimney, watching him as he meticulously nails down a line of fresh shingles. Balanced up here, I too get an inkling of that heady exhilaration that comes of inhabiting this distant high world reserved only for birds and madmen. In a way it's comforting, I'm thinking, knowing that summer or winter Perry is up here minding the roofs, stopping all those leaks and drips. In a way, I say. There is, however, something about his remoteness that makes me a little edgy—though I can't quite put my finger on what it is.

"Hey. Come on. Wake up. Don't go to sleep on me," he calls, hanging out over the edge by a toenail. "Bring down a bundle." Picking up a heavy stack of shingles, I gingerly ease my way toward him, trying not to look down over the edge. As he grabs the load from me in one hand, a gust of wind suddenly comes ripping down the valley. Feeling as though I'm going to be blown right off the roof, I desperately clamber back, reaching the chimney in the nick of time and hugging it for dear life.

"Shit," laughs Perry looking my way, standing with his feet casually planted at a crazy angle on the steep pitch. "Don't panic. The only ones that fall are the scared ones."

"I'm scared."

"Hey, you wanna make a quick fifty bucks?" he calls out.

"Up here?" I shiver.

"No. No. All you gotta do is put in a window."

"What kind of window?"

"Just a fucking window. You know, a picture window. It's easy. You should be able at least to do *that*."

"Don't *you* want the job?" I hedge.

"I thought you wanted work?" he says, a cigarette dangling from his mouth as he continues to nail. "Listen, don't ask so many goddamn questions. All you gotta do is cut a rough opening, frame it in and— Hey, you're not gonna fuck it up, are you?" he asks looking up, suddenly having second thoughts.

25

"Course not. Why should I?"

"Don't ask me. But listen, if I send you over, you *gotta* do a good job. I'm recommending you, if you know what I mean."

"Sure. I understand. Don't sweat it. You can count on me," I say, gratefully ringing up the fifty.

A few more tense loads to Perry and then we finally take a break, the two of us sitting down and lighting up cigarettes in the lee of one of the dormers. Perry takes a few thoughtful puffs while staring out into space and then suddenly turns to me and says, "Why the hell don't you leave Goobersville? You know you're not gonna find anything in this town."

"I still haven't exhausted every possibility."

"You should live in the city, Nudelman, that's where you belong."

"Yeah, with all those other New York City Jew types, huh?"

He laughs.

"And naturally I should sell you my house, right?"

"Naturally," echoes Perry who covets my nest in the woods, coming out whenever he can sneak away from his wife or a roof just to sit quietly in my kitchen, drink coffee, and watch the deer browsing in the field.

Yes, I agree huddling tighter against the chimney, he's right. Move. I should. But how can I leave when I know that after all these bitter months I've nearly made it to spring, that in a few short months I will hear that steady drip-drip of icicles, begin to smell the fresh earth, see the first spring flowers peeking up through the snow? And then know that sultry summer, tasty and warm and buzzing is just a few more quick months after that . . . Or that fall, crisp and bright and blue, is certain to follow. How, how can I leave now?

. . . . .

Before heading off to my window installation job this early gloomy morning, I am sitting in the kitchen assiduously studying a newspaper. Through the kind offices of my good friend Malvin Mandel (better known to his scientific colleagues as Dr. M.) I have become a regular recipient of *The New York Times.* This morning it is last week's Sunday Times that I'm reading though, considering my paltry state of affairs and the way I have fallen out of synch with the rest of civilized America, it could be last month's or last year's. Today, however, is a rare one since I am actually *reading* the print. Usually the paper is allowed to sit on the kitchen table together with the outgrown clothes that M's wife, Betty, has sent along for the kids—sit there alongside the plastic Baggies filled with the scraps from the Mandel's supper, bestowed upon us since they can't stand the thought of having a dog. Sometimes those Baggies lie there for days before I can draw myself away from watching the world suffocate in snow and toss the remains to my hound; my kids, having refined palates, still refuse to have anything to do with the Ms' leftovers. The Baggies do, however, tell an interesting tale. From them it is evident that in the Mandel household Spaghetti-Os and Campbell's Pork & Beans are the cuisine du jour. And, like the jingle says, "Campbell's in the cupboard's like money in the bank." One can't be too careful when only earning a measly forty grand a year.

"Is the inflation hitting you the way it's killing us?" asked Betty a couple of days ago when we met, her slender arms ladened with shopping bags.

Yes. *The New York Sunday Times.* I always begin with the financial section. Very informative, it is. The Times, it appears, is warning that as a result of the recent busyness boom and a far too rapid expansion we are—hold your belts folks!—in for a recession.

Anxiously I call Viveca over to read her the dire news. If up to now this has been a bonanza, I ask, gathering up my tools, what will the recession be like? Viveca is genuinely worried. I am fascinated. Here I thought I had plummeted to the very bottom of the pit, when, in actuality, all along I have been living in the bosom of moderate prosperity. My curiosity is utterly piqued so, as I drive towards town, putting a few more dangerous miles on my jalopy, held together with wire and twine and epoxy and chewing gum, I keep my eyes peeled for signs confirming the Times article. The drive to the Goobersville Heights address which Perry has given me takes me in toward the downtown from the south. It is a trip that leads me past shacks and claptrap buildings, low-slung boxes and trailers. I look and look, but as far as the eyes can discern I can detect no profound changes. Here in rural Goobersville life seems to continue on as ever—more Appalachian than even in Appalachia. At least there they have coal. Here, there has never been more than marginal farm land, soil which even the Indians didn't want. Here too, there is a bitter populace, one that has been jerked from farm to factory. And though the air in Goobersville is cold with dampness, it nonetheless seems to seethe with resentment. If ever there is to be a revolution, I am beginning to suspect it will not erupt on the campuses, nor will it spring from the ranks of disenfranchised blacks or well-intentioned liberals, it will emerge from places like this, good old Goobersville, where poverty is but thinly veiled and hostility for the rich and better educated festers like acne on a teenager's back. What's funny is that I never really saw it through all those years when times were good. Good, that is, for me.

As I continue my drive, rural Goobersville soon gives way to the suburbia of the city hills; shacks and run-down farms begin to fade into the pink and turquoise ranchburgers overlooking the flats. Down. Down. The road begins to descend into that Goobersville which lies on the valley floor trapped between the hills—the Goobersville University staring down on the city from its eastern heights, while on the opposite hill stands the famed Goobersville College of the Lower Intestine. The West Hill is purportedly residential, while on North Hill stands the munitions factory, laboring round the clock to turn out mortars, bazookas and bombs. And it is they, I am beginning to believe, and they alone who possess the ability to improve all this.

Finally I'm entering the downtown hodge-podge that was

ısed to be a pretty town. Today, however, it is a
۔۔۔ۮۑے of crumbling porches, tacked-on rooms and tarpaper
siding with only a few remaining isolated pockets of old
Victorian and Tudor homes that speak to me of an
esthetically happier era—gems hidden amidst the slum of
central Goobersville.

In truth I have come to loathe these trips, have learned to
minimize pain by training my eyes to rest only on discreet
oases—an old town hall, a doctor's office housed in a white
building of spires and towers and dormers, an old, elegant
hotel with funny white columns that has become a flop
house.

What a strange burg Goobersville is, I can't help but
think, waiting at a light and watching an undernourished
hill-woman dragging along her brood of five little tots with
running noses and rotted teeth, knowing as I do that up
there, on the hill at the Goobersville University, stuffy
academicians pass their time contemplating whether to
spend the coming summer in Nice or Athens or the Swiss
Alps where they will sip wine and attend a bogus math
conference. How disgusting. How utterly enviable. I can still
fondly recall those halcyon days when I, too, was a prince
receiving regular checks. The wind picks up and huge
snowflakes the size of cream pies smack against the
windshield. I am getting worried. Maybe it's as Dr. Mandel
says: I am becoming an anarchist.

The light finally changes and I pull myself back to the
business at hand—psyching myself up for my window job.

"But what do you know about putting in windows?" asked
Viveca last night when I popped the good news.

"What's there to know? I've built things before."

"Have you ever put in a window?"

"Oh Christ, stop giving me the third degree. Do you want
the money or don't you?"

"I'm just worried. It's in the Heights. You know what
those people are like up there. They're particular."

"So am I. Look, I'll do a good job. This'll probably lead
to other things, bigger things. Might even be the start of
a renovation business or something. You never can tell."

Fishtailing up the steep hill to fashionable Goobersville Heights, I check the address. 311 Willow Way. A couple of quick turns and I'm already on the right street. Very fancy area, if I may say so. Old stately stone houses and Victorians and contemporary jobbies in cedar and redwood. Quite a contrast to the rest of Goobersville. In this enclave live the crème de la crème of Goobersville. 301. 303. 305. The bankers and lawyers and car dealers and— Oh no! Damn it all! I groan, stopping in front of 311 and reading the name on the mailbox. Of all the people in the world, it turns out to be Gunz's house. Martin Gunz. Ex-colleague, professor emeritus, renowned child psychologist complete with German accent and beard—that miserable, patronizing, arrogant sonofabitch who was always convinced I would come to no good. I stop in front of the house and turn off the engine. Worriedly I fiddle with my tools. I hunt through my supplies as if hoping I forgot my hammer or something vital. Shit. How badly do I need the fifty? Badly. No. I absolutely won't go in. I start the car and begin to drive down the street. A couple of hundred feet and I'm again thinking about the money, about how much it can do. I make a U turn and head back. I can't futz around. I need the job. I'll just go in, quickly slam in the window, take my money and depart. I gather up my Skilsaw, extension cord and tool box and march up the long stone walk that has been meticulously cleared with snowblower and broom. Dr. Gunz's house, I can immediately see, is one of these old Victorians that has been authentically restored. Not a flake of peeling paint nor a missing touch to be found. Talk about perfection, I mutter ringing the doorbell and trying not to think of Martin Gunz.

The front door opens and there, standing in the doorway, is this crusty old lady with blue hair, built like a box with little sticks protruding for legs. One look at her face with its square jaw, Cro-Magnon forehead and reptilian eyes and I'm positive it's Dr. Gunz's old lady. Maybe I'm lucky, I'm thinking, looking beyond her into the apparently empty house. Maybe they're all away. I'll do the job and beat it before Gunz or his wife gets back.

"Hi. I'm the carpenter," I say, cheerfully holding aloft my electric saw as proof.

"You're late," she snarls.

"Yes. I know. I'm sorry. Weather was terrible. The roads are icy as—"

"Come in. It's blowing in. The heat," she says with Teutonic exactness, "it's all going out."

"Oh, yes," I step in quickly.

"Wipe your feet first."

"'Scuse me," says I, stepping out and wiping them.

"Here. You follow me," orders Commandant Gunz and dutifully I fall into lockstep as she proceeds over the wall-to-wall carpets, through the cavernous interior of this minor mansion.

"No, this way!" snaps elderly Frau Gunz as I manage to get lost, captivated by this palace of crystalline chandeliers and heavy German antiques.

"This is the window. Martin wants it here. Exactly here!" she points to the penciled markings on the wall of this rear room paneled in real oak that I suspect must be the good professor's study.

"Let me just see. I gotta make sure the studs are in the right place."

"Martin checked already. He knows where he wants it," says this utterly humorless tank on two legs, her bosom pressed forward and ready for attack.

For the sake of appearances I go to the wall and knock on it a few times, check out the hidden studs. Sure enough Dr. Gunz has done it right. "Perfect," I force a smile trying to melt this robot.

"Hmmpf," she answers and marches off.

I'm anxious to get this job done and over with, but on the other hand, I remind myself, thinking of Viveca's trepidations, I want to do it right. So, after lightly marking in the studs, I slip out the back door and check the siding on the outside. A quick measurement of the window stored in the garage and, sure enough, it's going to be easy pickings. I go back inside and lift up my power saw ready to start when in stalks the old lady.

31

"The floor!" she gasps, pointing to the trail that stretches from the rear door to the proposed window site.

"Oh. I'm sorry. I forgot to wipe my— Look, let me clean it up," I start to move toward her.

"No. Don't move an inch!" she cries, seeing new tracks. "Just stay there," she hisses, shoving newspaper under my feet.

"I may have to go back outside," I suggest timidly.

"Again?" she nearly pulls at her hair.

"Well, not right away," I say, deciding to try and work it from this end for the time being, hoping that I don't screw up on the outside.

A little more tidying up and Hausfrau Gunz finally disappears again. Relieved, I take a long, deep breath and carefully begin the task of tracing the outline of the hole I intend to cut. I am using my level to mark the exact horizontal cut when suddenly I'm interrupted by this heavy boring sensation at the back of my head. Slowly I turn and who do I see but Frau Gunz standing there behind me, tapping a toe, her hands on her hips.

"What have I done now?" I ask, meeting the piercing eyes of my accuser.

"Nothing . . . *yet*," she answers with polite candor.

Forcing a smile I turn back to my line, try to concentrate, but the old Gunz is making me very jittery. I attempt to draw the line, but my hands keep fumbling. Whenever I get the level in position I end up dropping my pen. Whenever the pen's under control the level starts drooping. I want to tell her to leave, get out of my hair, but, after all, this is her domain. And who am I but a lowly carpenter, I think, beginning to get a vague inkling of how that other woodworker must have felt a couple of thousand years earlier.

I plug in my saw and begin to cut cautiously into the paneling. In all my life as a professional carpenter I've never seen thick paneling like this; the going is slow and tough. A couple of feet of agonizing progress and I take a breather, turning around to discover the old lady standing there behind me busily vacuuming up the sawdust that's been flying all over. After she's sucked up every last speck, she turns off the vacuum cleaner and stands there glowering at me. I swear I'd really like to cut the rough opening without making sawdust, but it's a virtual impossibility. Fortunately, I think she understands.

Taking a deep breath I change blades, pick up my power saw and go back to cutting. Behind me I hear the vacuum cleaner starting up again. This time the sawing is going surprisingly fast. I'm making great progress when suddenly there's this big flash in front of my eyes just as a jolt of electricity shoots from my saw through my arms hurtling me backwards into Frau Gunz, causing me to bowl over the old lady and land, as fate would have it, smack on top of her with a little whoosh.

"Gott im Himmel. Was haben Sie angestellt!" she starts shouting, holding her chest and gasping for breath as I climb off her.

"Here. Let me help you up."

"What have you done!" she abruptly pulls away, refusing my offer to help wipe the sawdust off her dress.

"I don't know," I say, pale and still shaking from the jolt.

"Und the lights. The whole house. The electricity's gone!"

"I must have cut through a wire. Look, Miss . . . Mrs. . . . It's nothing serious," I explain, pursuing her as she rushes from room to room. "I just blew a little fuse. Maybe a couple. Maybe the main one. But it's nothing serious, believe me."

"Nothing serious?" she scoffs standing in the darkened house.

"Look, let me just finish the cut, then I can get at the wire. I'll reconnect it, we'll replace the fuse, and everything will be like new."

"So then hurry. What are you standing here for? The refrigerator's kaput. I have meat loaf in the oven. I want to do some ironing."

Hurriedly I pick up my Skilsaw and turn to the cut, only to discover that not only are her freezer, fridge, iron and stove out of commission, but also, naturally, my electric saw. For a moment I stand there smiling sheepishly, then, getting desperate, I pick up a chisel and hammer and frantically start whacking away at the wall, trying to gouge a hole where I suspect the wire is hidden. I'm getting a little over the line now and then, but if I can just get to that lousy wire and splice it, I'll be able to get this woman off my back.

A half hour later, soaked in sweat, chips of wood clinging to my face, I have finally carved an ugly gaping orifice into the wall and, sure enough, there's that little bugger of a wire sliced clean through. I strip the insulation, quickly twist and tape together the conductors and then, with a flickering candle in hand, stumble through the darkened basement hunting for the fusebox—knocking off the shelves, in the process, a whole line of home-canned beans, pickles and beets which I hastily clean up by shoving the broken glass and juicy vegetables under the shelves. Finally I find the fusebox, replace the burnt fuse, return the lights to the house. Relieved, I head back to my job only to discover a series of footprints marked in beet juice that has unfortunately followed me up from the basement.

I gotta get out of here, I warn myself, going great guns on the saw. With the old lady gone for the moment, I begin to work like a madman, zipping down the wood, banging and cracking out chunks of paneling. I'm tearing out insulation and knocking out the siding from the inside with a vengeance when, sure enough, the old lady appears again.

"Mein Gott!" she cries. "What's this?" she motions to the bloody footprints.

"In the dark, you see. I had a little accident," I begin to blubber, "I knocked over a little jar. Beets I think it was. But I don't think it will stain. My wife usually uses a little warm water, soap and—"

"Finish up and get out, for godssake!" she storms.

"That's what I'm trying to do. If you'll please just give me a chance and not stand on top of me," says I yanking on a board which not only comes off at the appointed line, but also rips loose an upper lip that in turn causes a bit of the ceiling to crack, a shower of white descending on the two of us. "Now please, don't get upset, it's nothing. Looks worse than it is. Just a little plaster. I'll fix it up just as soon as I'm

34

finished with the window. We'll paint it over and Martin will never even notice it. I promise. Really I do. Now, let's see, where was I?" I try making some idle conversation to take her mind off the ceiling. Christ, Viveca was right, I think, realizing that I'm going to have to hurry if I'm going to get out before Herr Doctor Gunz comes home and finds me in this terribly difficult situation. I'd really love to throw up my hands and leave, but I can't. I'm in too deep. Anyway, from here on it should be easy. I'll just stick in the window. Patch up the ceiling. And beat it.

Getting a bit rattled, I prop up a ladder on the outside and begin trimming my cut on the siding. I'm rushing the job, I'm afraid, and it's not coming out just precisely the way I had envisioned it. Something's not quite kosher, but I can't quite put my finger on it. The hell with it. Keep going. Get the window in and get out.

The new window is one of these fancy thermopane jobs with multiple louvres that can be opened by means of little widgets. Since it probably cost Professor Gunz a good five or six hundred dollars, I'm determined not to make the fatal error of damaging it. Under the continued watchful gaze of the old lady who pretends to busy herself in the kitchen, I gingerly carry the window from the garage toward the house. Dutifully I wipe my shoes, carry the bulky window through the livingroom, hallway and into the den—all without error. I lift the window up, press it against the opening and discover, to my swelling pride, that it actually fits. Not only fits, but does it perfectly. See there. I was right. And just look at the room. I mean besides the plaster and mess. It makes the study appear spacious and bright and cheery. What a change. What a view. A perfect setting for writing great papers on abnormal child development. I'm beginning to hastily toenail in the window, when I hear a car pulling up into the driveway. I check my watch. It's three-thirty. Three-thirty! And I haven't even been offered a morsel of food for lunch. No wonder I feel dizzy and exhausted. I hear the front door open. Voices. Oh-oh. A familiar one. It's Dr. Gunz. Home. Feverishly I begin finishing up the job, banging in nails like crazy. The ceiling

35

can wait. I'll come back tomorrow and patch it up when he's not around. The voices outside in the hallway are loud and excited.

"A carpenter?" I hear the old lady croak. "That's no carpenter. That's a wood butcher! You can't believe what's been going on."

Mumblemumblemumblemumble. I hear the deep, resonating baritone of Dr. Gunz, that man of patience accustomed to dealing with difficult children, trying to soothe his old distraught mother.

"Come, Mutti, let me see," I hear him approaching. Instinctively I turn my back and hunch over my work.

"Hmmmm. Let me see. What is happening here. Ah, the window . . . " he stands looking at it. "Ahmmm. Mister . . . Hallo?" he calls, trying to attract my attention. "Mister? Hallo?" he tries again and knowing that I am trapped, I slowly turn exposing my dirty, sweat-streaked face to Dr. Gunz who is still wearing his overcoat, one of those nice, thick, real fur coats with matching Russian-style hat.

"Nudelman!" he nearly plotzes in his pants. "You."

"Hi, Martin," I wave my hammer and smile weakly.

"But- but-" he stutters flushing, almost as embarrassed as I—old Frau Gunz's head swinging confusedly back and forth between me and her famous son.

"But what are you doing here?" he finally blurts out.

"Putting in a window," says I, trying to sound matter-of-fact, quickly gathering up my tools to beat a hasty retreat.

"Oh. I see," he says, still a little baffled looking up at that hole in his ceiling. 'Hmmm. Yes . . . The window . . ." he mutters and stands looking at it for the longest moment.

"But look, can't you see Martin, it's wrong," says Mommy Gunz being, as usual, a pain.

"Nothing's wrong," I try to reassure them, closing my tool box.

"Of course. Look Martin. Look at the line of the pictures. Ja? Now look at the window. It's . . . It's . . ."

"Yes . . . My goodness, I think it's leaning," says Dr. Gunz.

36

"No, it's *not* leaning," I try to wipe away their misgivings. I'm getting decidedly sick and tired of this job. Long hours, low pay, no chow.

"Let me see that level," he says, opening my box and helping himself to my tools. Then putting the level on the sill, he exclaims, "But yes. It *is* off!"

"My God, it's off a *fraction* of a millimeter. Nobody'll notice it."

"I notice it," says the old tank in blue hair.

"Christ, you'd notice *anything*."

"Now wait one minute here. That's my mother!"

"No kidding. I'd never have guessed. Delightful old lady you've got there."

"Why I've never—" begins to huff Mutti.

"Let me just tell you one thing. If the fucking window is off," says this workman, getting very touchy, "You can thank the old lady. She's been on my ass since the minute I came here."

"If you for one minute think—" begins Gunz pompously climbing onto his high horse.

"I think nothing. Listen, you two don't like the window?" I ask, picking up my hammer, Mutti reflexively raising her arms and ducking, "Well, we guarantee our work. You're not thoroughly pleased, huh? Then we'll just take it out. Like this!" I say smashing my hammer through the window, the welded glass exploding into a shower of fragments. "And maybe you don't like that one too, huh? Looks a little off to me," I say, pointing to another long one in the far corner.

"No! Stop!" they are screaming in unison.

"Nudelman!" Gunz is swelling up like a red blowfish, "Are you going crazy?"

"No trouble at all. We aim to please," says I, taking careful aim, whacking out the top and bottom in two quick strokes. "Now, anything else you people would like altered?"

Report #1 From the Group.

Those of us in the Group who have had the opportunity to observe Mr. Nudelman have been following his case with a great deal of interest. It is by now evident that Mr. Nudelman is subject to periods of dementia in which he appears to lose all contact with reality. Although actually impoverished, he frequently suffers delusions that he will imminently be wealthy. These periods of delusion are characterized by an insistence on buying drinks for friends of far better means, by sharing his meager rations of food with anyone who might drop by his house, and by being what is known as a "soft touch" for assorted beggars and panhandlers. A basic insecurity, resulting in a general debilitation of his ego support structure, renders Mr. Nudelman incapable of simply saying "no" during these characteristic seizures.

Paranoid tendencies are revealed in his recent allusions to understanding blacks, although the Group also has considerable evidence of a fully developed persecution syndrome in the subject.

Mr. Nudelman's proclivity for libidinous activity and his overstimulated curiosity in sexual matters must be viewed as overcompensation for the mother's love he felt deprived of in his youth. One facet of the subject's behavior that appears to be in his favor is his relative disinterest in women's breasts. Rather than being an indication of a libido balance, however, this should simply be attributed to repeated childhood exposure to his mother's over-sized mammaries that were forever spilling out of her blouse.

The subject's insistence upon the disintegration of our culture is, of course, a classic example of transference; his repeated references to the "breakdown of the economy," the "breakdown of the educational system," and the "breakdown of society" being no more than his feeble attempts to avoid recognizing that it is he, himself, rather than the "society," which is in the process of crumbling. Although the transference defense would seem to collapse in those lucid moments when the subject acknowledges that he is "a social misfit," it is always the "decaying social structure" which is considered to be awry in the warped mirror of his delusional desperation.

Examination of the subject's dietary preferences yields a good deal of insight into this disturbed personality. Although he drinks large amounts of milk, he has exhibited a clear preference for bakery goods, candies and syrups. He also uses extraordinary amounts of sugar on his morning cereal.

Sweets, which can readily be equated with reward and the need for approval, are the food of choice of the precarious and imperiled psyche. These preferences, coupled to his desire for creamy types of ingestions (ice cream, custards, puddings, sour cream, whipped cream filled chocolate eclairs) which are physiologically mammary in content and psychically soothing in effect, are further indications both of this longing for his mother (despite his vehement protestations to the contrary) and his most desperate need to stabilize an otherwise quirky mental state. His nearly obsessive compulsion for lobster (usually taken with drawn butter), fresh shrimps and other seafoods may simply be gustatory in origin, but does warrant further examination.

Prognosis: His refusal to even consider psychiatric help, proclaiming it a luxury of the middle and upper classes, precludes any hopes for a complete recovery. His attempts at self-treatment, as well as his obsessive writing and self-examination can only worsen an already deteriorating condition. What Mr. Nudelman needs, in the opinion of this experienced group, is professional care.

As has been pointed out in our preliminary profile, his behavior is largely anti-social. Most of his attempts at employment may be characterized as self-defeating. His delusion of being able to write for a living is severely destructive. That he is violence prone is borne out by his repeatedly expressed secret desire to murder his teenage neighbor, George Szorsky, simply because the youth was harassing him with his hi-fi, tearing up Nudelman's lawn with his tractor, and threatening the lives of Nudelman's children on a few isolated occasions.

Recommendations: In lieu of immediate confinement, the Group would like to advocate the following treatment:

1) That Mr. Nudelman be prevented from writing any further harangues against his circle of acquaintances, our economic system, society, or the American way.

2) As exhibited in his perennial pooh-poohing of the work ethic, as well as in his contempt for the wealth of fine products manufactured by our modern technology, Mr. Nudelman has demonstrated that he obviously thinks he's too good for most types of "ordinary" jobs. However, solely for his own benefit, we strongly urge the initiation of an effective regime of reality therapy—that Mr. Nudelman be forced to undertake the most humiliating employment, if only to temper his spirit and bring him back into the fold of normal society.

3) That our careful monitoring and surveillance of his behavior continue unabated and that in our next report, time permitting, we should devote ourselves to examining some of the characteristics and nuances of his obsessive-compulsive "literary" attempts.

40

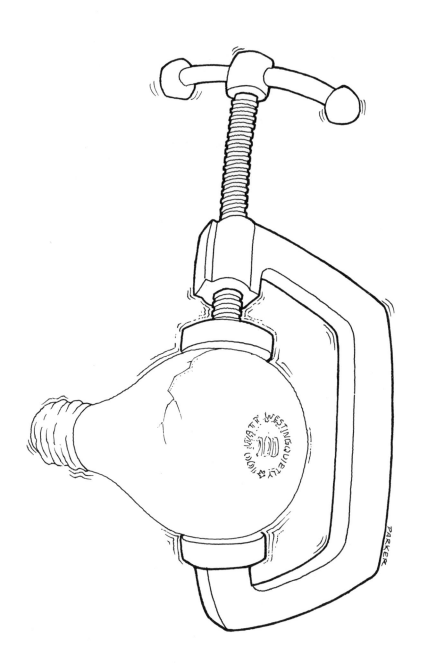

The heavy snow that's been falling all day has finally turned to a flurry and I am outside digging clear the front of the house. The late afternoon sun begins to peek through the breaking clouds, flooding the snow with a pale yellow. As I shovel I can't help but feel a sense of peace until, that is, I notice the sound of an unfamiliar car driving past the Szorskys'. Hearing the motor stop, I sneak up a small knoll and peer down through the trees to discover a Sheriff's car parked at the beginning of our road. With pounding heart I lie on the snow and watch as this fat deputy clutching a piece of paper gets out of the car, surveys my road and, shaking his head, begins waddling through the nearly crotch-deep snow. I'm hoping against hope that this lawman will give up as other visitors have before him, but this pudgy little individual is stubborn and as he begins to near the house, I quickly dart back between the trees.

"Listen, Viveca," I say, trying to catch my breath. "There's a deputy Sheriff coming."

Viveca's eyes widen.

"Now, don't panic. If he's looking for me, just tell him I'm not here. You haven't seen me. In weeks!"

"What have you done?"

"Nothing. Nothing at all. Look, I can't stand here going into long explanations. He'll be here any second," I give her a quick peck on the cheek, disappear into the root cellar and bury myself among the potatoes and turnips.

Waiting. Waiting. I hear the deputy lumber up the stairs to the house. A loud knock. Viveca opens the door—a little too fast in my opinion, especially for someone not expecting a visitor.

"I'm looking for Neil Nudelman," pants the deputy.

42

"He's not here," says Viveca faintheartedly.

"When do you expect him back?"

"I . . . I don't know . . . I haven't seen him in a couple of weeks . . . I think he's on the West Coast," she says very unconvincingly. "But what's the matter?"

"Got a warrant for his arrest."

"A what?" Viveca nearly dies.

"Would you please call us at this number as soon as he gets back," the deputy hands her a card.

"But what did he do?"

"Just call us," answers the lawman, turning and looking disgustedly back at the distance he has just trudged.

After the cop leaves, I dust myself off and go up to face Viveca.

"I think I deserve an explanation," fumes Viveca still red-faced from lying. For some atavistic reason, Swedes have this disgusting, inherent respect for the law.

"It's really nothing. Just a little misunderstanding, I suspect, with the Gunzs," I say, and go on to explain how I may have accidentally done a little damage to the Gunzs' house while trying to install that ill-fated window.

.   .   .

Is *Goobersville Breakdown* about the breakdown of Goobersville or about my impending breakdown?

Of late, sleep has become more elusive than ever and the dreams that I do have when it finally arrives are vivid and frightening. Last night, for instance, I dreamt that I had parasites. They (whoever it was that opened my intestines) showed them to me. They were little bugs the size of dimes with hundreds of hair-like legs and they were running around everywhere. When I woke up, I found that I was sick to my stomach.

I got out of bed and after three cups of coffee, finally managed to look at myself in the mirror. I stared into my own eyes and saw in them a ghastly look. What was it? I

43

went over to Viveca, bent down and had her examine my eyes.

"What do you see when you look into them?" I asked.

"Despair," she said knowingly.

Despair. Do others see it too when they look in my eyes or is it only Viveca? Surely they must see it. And more. Apathy. It has to be. It's the only defense against vulnerability, the gas that seeps in to fill the vacuum when hope has escaped.

.　　.　　.

Happy Days. I have work, but better yet I will have income. Hallelujah and praise the Lord. Thank you, Jesus and a special thanks to brother Bernard Kaufman who, in this time of urgent need, has come forth with an offer of employment to this most humble and humiliated of human beings. I fall on my knees, rattle my rosary and trace the Star of David across my navel. Well, so maybe it isn't really employment, but it is income. Temporary? Sure, but isn't everything? A man dying of kidney failure, cancer and priapism must learn to be grateful for tiny reprieves, I keep reminding myself as I begin my literary labors for brother Kaufman. Two dollars a page is two dollars a page. Sure it's prostitution, but this is wartime and I must walk the streets to feed my babies.

Through Mr. Z., an elderly gent I have known for many years, I have been introduced to brother Kaufman. Mr. Z. may be the only illiterate literary agent in New York City, may have lungs of brown from which he is forever bringing up sputum, may have unique ideas for books that are utterly worthless (he wants me to do a cookbook entitled "Famous Last Meals") but he's a real *Mensch* with a heart of gold.

Yes. Brother Kaufman. We are in Luchow's in lower Manhattan. He is sitting puffing on the end of a golden cigarette holder, a diamond ring on his pinky, as I, hunched

44

over the table, shovel in pound after pound of Sauerbraten and dumplings, hot rolls dripping in butter, Wursts and Eisbein. While I am busily making a pig of myself at Brother Kaufman's expense, he is rattling on about his literary achievements. He has published *two* books already—one about how to acquire and destroy companies, the other a description of how he became a millionaire at the expense of his former partner. Nodding with feigned attention, I am stealthily picking the last crumbs off the white linen tablecloth and letting them surrepticiously find their way into my mouth.

"Did you have a chance to read *Heaven Bent, Hell Bound?*" he asks, referring to the box of typewritten pages sitting between the Kartoffelsalat and Schnitzel.

Thoughtfully I lean back in my chair, rub my chin, stare at the ceiling, scratch my head.

"I've examined it with a good deal of interest," I remark staring him right smack in the eye. I still haven't exactly read it, but my answer is not quite a lie. I have examined it, even though cursorily—and where there is money there most certainly has to be interest. Ask any bank.

"And?" he asks anxiously, probing my eyes . . . Does he see?

And. Yes. Ah-hem. Well . . . I look at Bernard Kaufman, asking myself if I can go through with this. Kaufman is in his mid-fifties. His skin is smooth and clean shaven, tanned though it is mid-winter, his suit is well cut, his tie of imported silk, his shoes have a mirror polish. But even aside from all the icing, Mr. Kaufman possesses that well-fed, never worried look, that air of surety that tells all, says that on the day he was born, eased with jelly out of his mother's vagina, he already knew that he was destined to control his own gigantic ad agency, to play monopoly with real property. Whereas someone like myself is always living with nerves on the surface, raw and exposed, people like Mr. Kaufman, like Mandel and his lovely wife, seem to wander

45

through life unscathed, happily oblivious to all the pain of the world. And I envy them, I do.

I look across the table, still stalling for time, look at Kaufman. His eyes are clear and blue and determined. Whereas I have become frazzled and worn about the edges, his lines are still sharp and clear. Whereas I am plagued by second thoughts, he is a man utterly devoid of internal conflict. He has acquired companies with the ease with which other men wipe their noses. He has taken over entire industries without a drop of capital—his is the face that inspires confidence, that can even make a suspicious banker part with droves of his treasured dollars.

Bernie (we are already on first name terms—this is, after all, a democratic country) has everything and anything he could ever want. His speech and manners are impeccable and put me to shame; he is anything but the stereotype of a Jew. Yet. Yet. There is *one* weakness. Though he can run circles around the stock markets, corner pork-bellies or spring chickens, can create fortunes out of thin air, he still has not quite achieved his final goal of being a recognized author. A small thing, perhaps, but a writer he must be. Although he has conquered the world of means and beans, Bernie Kaufman has still not quite acquired a controlling share of the arts. And that is why we are here; why I am eating myself to illness to the accompaniment of an oompah band now tooting out a lively German polka.

"Have you considered rewriting it yourself?" I suggest, skirting the issue.

"Well I would, except that I'm working on two other novels, and I'd rather keep going forward than stop to go backwards."

"Yes. Forward." I nod in understanding. More novels! This man could prove to be a veritable gold mine. Nudelman, for Godsake, be careful what you say. Lie a little. So you think his fiction is a pile of shit? Who are you to judge? For all you know you may be sitting across from

46

another Joyce or Shakespeare, a Malamud with a diamond pinky ring, an Isaac Singer disguised as a dandy. Talent. Speak about 'talent.' Everyone's got 'talent.' Even Hitler had a certain talent.

"Would you care for dessert?" asks the waiter, clearing off the dishes.

"No, we'll just have coffee," says Kaufman, waving him away.

"What do you have?" I inject with delicate speed. Yes. Strudel sounds delightful. Apfelkuchen? Maybe a little ice cream on top. Though I should watch those calories, you know. Ah, how I wish I could stuff a little of all this in my pocket and sneak it home to Viveca who loves good food.

"Well," asks Kaufman again, turning back to me. "What did you think of it? I want your *honest* opinion. Mr. Z. recommended you highly."

"I was sort of taken with it. Read it with a good deal of interest," I nod biting my tongue. Interest? Keep going, don't stop. Talk about the talent. "There's no question about the talent," I say and watch Mr. Kaufman light up like a Christmas tree.

"Mr. Z. said it needed a little bit of touching up, sort of a fine tuning, a few changes here and there," he says and then quickly adds, "Though if you want to make major changes, you certainly may. Anything to get it in publishable form. I could do it myself, but I'm in such a rush," says Mr. K. and then goes on to confess about his obsession: writing. Every free moment, when he's not creating an ad for vaginal deodorants or swapping companies, he's at his desk writing, writing, writing. "It can become obsessive," he laughs at himself, and suddenly I am frightened. If Mr. Bernard Kaufman, author of *Hell Bent, Heaven Sent,* who cannot write a decent sentence, is convinced without the slightest doubt that he is a writer, maybe . . . maybe I, too, have been 'writing' under the same illusions. Kaufman goes on to describe the symptoms—the mind always working on plots, the eyes that are always observing, the mid-sleep assaults of

47

ideas, the pad of paper left ready at his night-table. Perhaps I have been deluding myself all these years?

So what! B.F.D. Big Fucking Deal. It still doesn't solve the problem of child support. Money, Money, Money. Keep your eye on the ball.

"Do you think it's publishable?" asks Mr. K., who a moment ago was so certain it was. Aha! So he does have creeping little doubts.

"In its present form?" I ask. He nods. "No." Ah, such pleasure to be able to tell the truth.

"And if you worked on it?"

"I couldn't guarantee anything. And I wouldn't want to give you false hopes. I think that if we could come to some . . . some arrangement . . . restructure . . . fix up sentences . . . modify the plot . . ."

"Yes. Yes. Yes," he is smiling.

"I thought, well, how about opening with Pete lying naked on his . . ."

. . .

Two dollars a page is two dollars a page. And there are four hundred of them. Two months of good living, I reason now, back at home and staring out the window. Out in the distant Szorsky field I can see three deer making their way through the snow up the steep incline. Thanks to me and my lousy gun, one of the deer is hobbling. It will continue to hobble through the winter, a constant reminder of my blunder.

I have set up a schedule. Five pages a day, an absolute maximum of a half hour spent on any one page—hopefully I will be able to get away with less. Two and a half hours, maybe three, in the early morning for Brother Kaufman, three hours in the afternoon of writing for myself. I've only managed to rewrite three of Bernie's pages and already my mind is beginning to drift. How am I going to clear four hundred?

48

As our story opens Pete Miller, alias Bernie Kaufman, is standing naked in front of Sylvia, an Eastside call-girl who is on her knees busily sucking Pete's peter. With the index finger of her right hand up his asshole, and her left hand voluptuously (his word) squeezing his balls, Pete is coming in her mouth in gobfulls of hot sperm that shoot out faster than she can swallow them. "Oh, Pete, Pete," she is crying in ecstasy as he ejaculates, Sylvia hungrily licking up the sticky mess and begging for more of his tasty nectar.

All this is not only ridiculous, but a physical impossibility. I should know. I used to be a physicist. How in God's name can she talk with a full mouth? How can she greedily "lick up his love juice" when her mouth is fully occupied? If she sticks her tongue out, it'll all pour out.

I call up Bernie. Collect.

"Go ahead and do whatever you think needs to be done," he says, giving me a free hand.

"Anything?"

"Anything," he says, explaining that he's already started on the outline of novel number four and can't be bothered with details.

I return to the story with my carte blanche. Who knows, I begin to wonder, maybe this is the kind of fiction that really sells? Maybe Brother Kaufman really understands the literary market? Maybe this will make the *New York Times* best seller list, will be a *Book of the Month Club* selection. He certainly can't do any worse than I've done . . . I also suspect I'm beginning to believe my own lies.

As I delve into *Hell Sent, Heaven Went* I'm beginning to get the hang of the story. As the novel develops, Pete Miller, businessman and wheeler-dealer who has already made three fortunes, is destined to fuck his way across one ocean and two continents, all with prostitutes, all of whom, like lovely Sylvia, will refuse payment because Pete is such a magnificent lover. With his rapturous cock he will break hearts and hymens (now *there's* the title! "Hearts and

49

Hymens") and it will be his undoing. His wife, who has been sitting home knitting all this time, will discover his exploits and threaten to leave him; his partner will start embezzling while Pete is taken up with his genitals; his empire will begin to crumble. Only in the last minute will Pete understand what has transpired, how his life of depravity is leading to his ruin. As the story closes, Pete has come home to his wife and is busy engaging in (for once) good, old-fashioned position number one to his wife's chorus of "Fuck me, Pete, fuck me, hard."

It all makes no sense and yet it all makes perfectly good sense. Sure the sentences ain't English and the action is ludicrous, but there it is—three hundred and ninety-seven pages to go. How in God's name am I ever going to make it?

.   .   .

This afternoon after picking up Leif and Magnus from the school bus, I check my mailbox and find amidst the assorted bills an airmail envelop plastered with colorful Chinese stamps. Eagerly I open the letter.

Mr. Neil H. Nudelman
One Mt. Nudelman Rd.
Goobersville, New York

Dear Mr. Nudelman,
   Thank you for your letter to Chairman Mao expressing your deep interest in our country. I regret to inform you that our beloved Chairman died over two years ago.

Respectfully yours,

Feng Wa Wei

Feng Wa Wei
Fourth Deputy Minister
People's Bureau of Information

After reading and rereading this disheartening news I

decide to cheer myself up by glancing at the newspaper in Maud's box. I'm sure that Mrs. Szorsky—who reads only the funnies and accident reports—won't mind my taking a little peek. I slip the paper out of her box, unfold it and there, on the front page, is an enormous picture of Martin Gunz staring out at me.

NOTED CHILD PSYCHOLOGIST DEAD

Feverishly my eyes begin to scan the article. Famed Goobersville University professor. Died unexpectedly last night at age sixty. Of a heart attack. University community and town shocked by unexpected passing. Mother to accompany body back to Schwabing, Germany for burial in family plot. No flowers. Family would appreciate donations to Wilhelm Schnitler Foundation For The Study of Aberrant Child Development.

I hear the kids calling to me to hurry up, but I can't budge. I just stand there, still clutching that paper, transfixed by the picture of Martin Gunz . . . Of a heart attack, I mutter, thinking back to how that vein at the side of his forehead bulged when I started going after his windows. A heart seizure, I feel my own heart beginning to palpitate arrythmically . . . Maybe it was all my carryings on that killed him, I begin to fret. The logical side of me says that if he was going to die of a heart attack, a little aggravation (which he deserved) doesn't matter a bit. The other side of me warns that if it wasn't for me and my stupid temper, he might still be alive today . . . Then, of course, there is that third side which says that with Gunz out of the way and Mutti off to Schwabing, the complaint and arrest warrant he probably signed may have no validity . . . Which means I may be off the hook.

Poor Gunz, I am thinking, catching up with the boys who are happily trading snowballs, oblivious to this unexpected passing. Even if he was a pompous bore, Martin Gunz was still a human being, a man who wanted to go on living. Maybe I should go to the library and read one of his books?

51

Justifiable homicide. Surely there must be extenuating circumstances when in the eyes of the law, murder is forgivable. Something akin to a shooting feud has broken out with the Szorskys just when I most need peace to be able to concentrate on Bernie's best seller. What now? Do we call the police again or do I kill the Szorsky boy? Oh, I swear I could put a bullet right between his eyes and do a jig as the blood gushes out of the hole. If ever there was a time I was capable of murder it is today. I am livid with anger; my pen shakes. Like a festering sore, seventeen-year-old George Szorsky has erupted to the surface—his cyclic outbursts bringing infection and pus to our lives, each paroxysm more dangerous than its predecessor. To call the police is only to fuel the fires and court even further disaster. Besides, even with Gunz too dead to press charges, there is still a warrant out for my arrest. To remain silent is to submit to abuse heaped upon abuse, insult that could bring even a saint to gnashing his teeth.

Angry, hostile, fatherless Georgy Szorsky, Polish peasant of seventeen has gone on the rampage again just as I'm ready to attack page number four. He has been tuned in, waiting for precisely this unique opportunity.

But before I murder this obnoxious creature, perhaps a bit of history is in order, a dash of psychological and geographical insights.

The Szorsky clan consists of mother Maud, ringleader and drill-press operator; Henry, a thirty-three-year-old teenager and purported eunuch; Irma, an avid thirty-year-old horse humper and dedicated spinster; and, of course, George, that all-American calf buggerer—all fine upstanding, church-going Catholics, they are. When last surveyed, the Szorskys owned sixty acres, but as they have come to realize so astutely, sixty acres ain't hardly enough space for their wide range of activities. As a result the Szorskys have spread themselves over the Goobersville mountains, spilling over their boundaries like a fat ass on a bar stool. With their minibikes and snowmobiles, tractors and mudbikes, horses and cows, the Szorskys eagerly rip up and litter the land, bringing down upon all and sundry their own special brand of erosion and havoc. Their horses and cows aimlessly wander along the highway causing near fatal accidents. Letting her barnyard buddies graze in the neighbors' flower beds and gardens has provided insightful mother Maud with the opportunity to see the people about her for what they really are. "What kind of stinkin' neighborhood is this, anyway?" screeched Maud one bright spring morning, shaking her beakish head and pointing down the road. "Why that—that *witch* down the road called the *Sheriff!* First they come and, kind as you please, help themselves to our manure, then they go and call the police! The police!" screamed Maud, her contralto reverberating across the valley.

I think it was two summers ago that the first of the serious incidents occurred (as if previous years were tranquil). It began with little Georgy, mother's angel, being bored. No one was home. Mama and Irma and Henry were out working in the factory. Apparently tiring of masturbating and building gas engine planes, Georgy took his brother's monstrous hi-fi speakers and, beaming them at our house on the hill, began the first in a series of acid rock concerts. Day after day we feigned deafness. Chipmunks complained of migraines. The robins began laying broken eggs. We decided to ignore it, hoping, that like a case of syphilis, it might just go away.

"Maud, please," broken, I finally entreated on bended knee, "He's driving us crazy!"

"Can't do nothing about it. That boy won't listen to me," she shrugged her shoulders.

"What am I supposed to do?"

Maud shrugged again. She shrugged as she shrugged when finally one of her wandering horses got hit by a car—the horse rolling over once and walking casually away from a demolished VW. Shrugged as she did when her half-witted son, Henry, by mistake leveled the trees on another neighbor's land. But it was the trees' fault for being there, reasoned Maud, just as the assaults on our property have been our fault for deciding to have a garden, flower-beds or lawn, just as the others will forever be in her debt for having once accepted a cartload of horseshit.

Once, two summers ago, I foolishly tried for justice and called the Sheriff's office. What a joke, I laughed to myself. I, thief of pens and paperclips and long distance calls, turning to the police for help. And they came with the speed of a plague, ready, willing and able to defend my rights.

"O.K., turn it off!" commanded the Goobersville deputy who so obviously hated teenagers, his forehead wrinkling in pain from the pounding speakers—African aborigines invading the pleasant appleblossomed hills of Goobersville.

"But it isn't against the law to listen to music, is it?" meekly asked the Jackson boy, attracted by the music from down the road.

"Who are you?" snarled the deputy.

"Me?"

"Yeah you!"

"Rick."

"Rick what?"

"Rick Jackson."

"What are you doing here?" he cross-examined the kid as I secretly hugged myself in ecstasy.

"I'm a friend."

"Then keep your mouth shut un'erstand!"

"I was just—"

54

"I said shut up and I meant it!" shouted the deputy above the din, eyeing Georgy who stood with a nasty taunting grin on his face, his arms belligerently folded.

"Well, are you gonna turn it off or not?"

Georgy stood motionless, without so much as batting an eye. What goes on in that blond head behind those beady eyes, I wondered. Is this a stance for the benefit of his friend, or is he truly unintimidated by the cops? Does he equate the police with his mother who, after ranting and raving, inevitably gives in and then goes out to buy him a new bandsaw or minibike?

"Look, you're breaking the law," I inject, hoping that he will not force my hand. "You can be arrested and stuck in jail. Right?" I ask and the cop nods, rattling his handcuffs.

"If this gentleman signs a complaint, I'll arrest you for harassment," snarls the deputy.

"I don't care," muttered Georgy, giving that Szorsky shrug, that graceful movement in which the shoulders are first rolled up and then forward, the face tilted slightly to one side, a sour expression achieved by a special pursing of the mouth muscles which causes a lower ignorant lip to protrude. And what was going on in that little booger's mind? Georgy was, of course, just employing Szorskian logic: it is my ears, not his electronics that are causing the trouble. If he is arrested it will be solely by mistake, the courts and his mother will exonerate him. Georgy vindicated, I will sit in jail.

Then suddenly the cop moved in, three hundred pounds of police authority waddling with wonderful agility toward the boy, handcuffs and holsters and mace and god-knows-what dangling over the deputy's ass.

Ah, how I would simply have loved to see Georgy sitting in the Goobersville prison, or even Attica or Sing-Sing. I ain't particular. Yet I couldn't indulge my delicious whims. Were Georgy to be arrested by me, it would be an invitation for the rest of the S. clan to close ranks and join in a feud that would stretch off into eternity. Also, I am dangerously vulnerable, as Maud is inclined to hint. The road leading to our house on the mountain passes in front of their farm and is owned at that point by them. It is the strategic Mitla Pass. I am landlocked and, given sufficient enmity, they are fully capable of cutting off our access. At that moment I was not in a position to make the downpayment on a helicopter.

As the cop moved in, flushed and lusting for combat, a minor miracle took place: Georgy suddenly relented. He pulled the plug. As easy as that. Thunder yielded to deathly stillness. I sighed and smiled and blessed the entire Goobersville constabulary.

"But O.K. for you Charlie," warned Georgy, eyeing me with Polish daggers as I turned to leave.

A threat? I smiled benignly—a mature adult gazing indulgently down on an obstreperous child. And I gave him a shrug.

The walk up the mountain was heaven. Quiet. Utter, wonderful stillness. Once again I could hear the birds chirping in the trees, hear the wind whistling through the pines, hear the airplanes droning above.

I lay down on the warm grass in front of my house and studied a fly buzzing round my head. I yawned. Closing my eyes I began to doze, yummy sleep just ready to overtake me when the air was shattered by the starting of a nearby engine. I bolted upright. There, but feet away and revving up big brother's new chain saw, stood Georgy Szorsky beginning the task of dropping each and every tree in front of our house but still conveniently on *his* side of the border. Down came the apple trees that gave luscious fruit each fall. Down the long, elegant oaks and the maples and the choke cherries.

For thirty agonizing minutes I watched as George Szorsky, cool as a moose, completed his task, leaving our house naked and exposed on a flank—the rotting trunks still lying there today—fair game for Maud's prying eyes.

56

Yes. Shooting feud. Justifiable homicide. Now, with the stage set and by means of excerpts from my daily journal, I will try to recreate the latest socio-political chapter of Szorskian history:

MONDAY: A winter thaw. The snow has turned to slush and the creeks are running again. On the southern slope there's even a bit of earth showing. A warm break and as sure as you can smell manure behind the Szorsky barn, my dear neighbors are already up to something. Irma, that great horse-lover, decided late last week to park her three crazy nags smack in the middle of our road. To drive up toward the house we must stop where the horses stand parked, get out and shove on their asses, and then try to quickly sneak through, usually getting stuck in the slush.

For five days through this January thaw, the horses have stood in rain and sleet and melting snow, tethered to a scant foot of rope. The line so tight they can barely move their heads, the horses stand locked in place, their hooves tearing up my road, churning it into waist deep mud—the same road that I endlessly labor on with pick and shovel.

Shall I complain and risk all that comes with it?

TUESDAY: Another day of watching my road being ravaged, my labors undone. Were it cold, then at least there would be solid ice under their hooves instead of thawing earth. The mud is so bad that we can barely make it through.

Screw it! I must forget the road and concentrate on my new found employment.

WEDNESDAY: It's unfair. They simply don't have the right to destroy my work. It is the story of our years as neighbors. I plant and clean up, they destroy and litter. Bottles on the road that cause flats; empty, jagged cans left behind on which the kids trip or cut their feet. If only I had a bazooka, I could wipe them out. A couple of mortars. Maybe I should poison their horses? No. The animals are innocent. I should poison the Szorskys, that's what I should do.

THURSDAY: Even placid Viveca is bugged. Aha, so it's not just hypersensitive me. They *are* pricks. Oh, just to have a little grenade—toss the pineapple through their window like in the WWII flicks. If this were wartime I could level their place with impunity. I could denounce them. Come to think of it Georgy wouldn't even be around, he'd be drafted. And the horses would be inducted for military service. Haha. Very funny. It still doesn't get rid of those critters.

Try to forget. Forget it? How can I? Every time we drive home we are reminded. Every time I look out the window I see them grinding away at my road.

FRIDAY: Enough is enough. I have gone down to the Szorskys, red-faced though controlled. They are all sitting around the kitchen table engaged in dinner. Henry, stooped over his soup, looks up as I enter. They all look up at the intruder. Excuse me. Bla. Bla. Nice weather. Feels like spring. Apropos nothing. Would you mind moving the horses?

Maud looks up and with a rivulet of soup running down the side of her chin proceeds to give a Szorskian shrug. Ain't her horses. Ain't mine, says brother Henry. Not mine, said the little pig. Not mine, said the goose. And Irma, owner of the culprits, what does she say? Not a fucking word. Not a shrug. Not even a burp. Nudelman shuffles out, a nigger among whites, a Jew amongst hill people. I am waiting. Any day they are likely to yell dirty Jew—except that I have led them to believe I am a Christian and it is Viveca, the foreigner from Sweden, who is obviously the Jew.

SATURDAY: Let sleeping dogs lie and dozing horses stand. I would like to ignore the undermining of my road, but for nearly a week it has been galling me, burrowing into my intestines and muscles like a trichina worm. I've been unable to progress even a single page on Bernie's book. My work and income have been suspended mid-scene. For nearly a week Pete Miller has been standing with his erect penis poised before some orifice—I'm so confused I forget which or whose. How am I going to keep the story line straight with these horses destroying my sanity? Bernie even called this morning, wanted to know how it's going.

"I'm very excited to see the rewrite," he chirped after I told him I was on chapter three. Bernie's already starting on his nineteenth book, or whatever it is, and I can't get beyond *page* three. Last night I had a dream that Bernie drove up from New York to see the finished pages. Fortunately his Cadillac got mired right in the mud by the horses and he never made it to the house.

SUNDAY MORNING: The Szorskys are now in church. Father Goodness, or whatever-the-fuck his name is, is telling them how to be good Christians. Tell them how to be good neighbors, that's what you should tell them! Tell them how to be decent, compassionate human beings, you dumb, god-fearing sonofabitch!

Shows you how mad I am—I'm even cursing a priest, a personal messenger of God. Probably some nice old rosy-cheeked man who passes each Sunday explaining to his flock how I crucified their savior. I'm so mad I could crucify Maud and shove a crown of thorns up her cunt.

SUNDAY AFTERNOON: I have thrown caution to the wind and moved the horses myself—no easy operation, that. The road was already finished—in the spring I will have to re-dig and re-ditch that stretch—but I'd be damned if I was going to let it go any further.

Cautiously I approached the first horse—the steed clearly stir-crazy from being confined to the same tiny plot of earth for nearly two weeks. His coat was caked with mud and as I neared him he nervously flattened his ears. Then suddenly, unaware that I was really his ally, he lashed out at me with his hind hooves trying to catch me in the balls. Easy boy. Atta horse. I talked to him like they do in the cowboy pictures and after ten minutes and a few more attempted

59

hoofings things looked real cool, as they say. I even thought I had him eating out of my hand when suddenly he bit me on the shoulder. Pure Szorsky vindictiveness, that's what it was. But I won. It was no easy victory, but in the end anger proved the determining factor and I started on the other two horses. By comparison, the first one turned out to be a lamb.

An hour later, drenched in nervous sweat, I climbed the long stairs to my deck and collapsed.

"He moved the horses!" I hear Maud's melodious voice echoing up the hill. Very astute. I think she noticed that the horses are back in her barn where they belong.

"That dumb father of yours moved *our* horses!" she shrieks like the bird of prey she is.

Oh-oh. The kids are down there.

"With his dumb hands he moved our horses. Tied them so tight they can't even move their heads. You tell him bla bla bla."

Half an hour later the boys are back all excited.

"Mrs. Szorsky says—" begins Leif, all breathless.

"I know. I know. Just ignore her."

"And Georgy says he's coming up with his tractor and says you better move the car out of the way or he'll yank it out!" says Magnus worriedly knitting his eyebrows.

"Relax. Just ignore them. Don't listen to what—"

I hear the sound of an approaching tractor. By the time I reach the window, Georgy and his juggernaut are already well past my car and are barrelling along the road that continues around and circles our mountain. Obviously he is hell bent on tearing up the back section of road that I seeded only last fall, and he is doing it solely because I've asked him not to.

The trail around our property is a serene path that cuts through the narrow pass separating my hill from the Szorsky land. Untouched, the road has developed a lovely mosaic of mosses and ferns. In spots it is cut by tiny brooks that gurgle year round with icy spring water. In a rare moment of cooperation the Szorskys and I have jointly pulled huge stumps across the far end of this road to block access from the rear. For Maud it was a move to keep out the "drunks" who live in the back (a fear I planted in her head). For me it was, in fact, to keep the *heathens* (as they are locally known) from tearing up the trail with their jeeps and mudbikes.

But it is on the front lines, not from the rear that the attack has come. It is the devout churchgoers, not the heathens who are the enemy, I belatedly realize as Georgy grinds up the hill—Georgy who cares naught for his sister's horses, who cares even less whether or not seeds grow, but whose sensitive antennae have been eagerly sifting the airwaves waiting for the right signals.

Quickly I dash down the stairs and cut through a corner of the woods to head him off.

"Wait!" I call out, the voice of reason in the wilderness, standing midroad.

Perched on his pulsing stallion, Georgy glares down at me with venomous eyes. "What do you want?" he snarls.

"This has nothing to do with you."

"Get out of my way, will ya? This is our road too."

"I know it is."

"Hurry up, I'm wasting gas," he says, dying to run me over.

"Georgy," I plead looking into a pair of blue eyes that have turned vacant with hate. "You know I've seeded the road—"

"I don't care," he dully intones.

"But I do. At least give it a chance to grow."

"I don't care."

"Look, Georgy, you have nothing to do with those horses. Now you're smarter than the rest of them."

Georgy sighs, tapping his foot impatiently on the brake as the machine continues to roar, eager to take off, its tires almost as tall as I stand.

"Leave the road alone. If you care at all about our friendship," I say, trying to invoke the times he has been sane and eager to talk, eager to show off that new remote control plane that cost Maud one-hundred and fifty dollars.

"If you don't like it, get out! MOVE!" he hisses through gritted teeth and the machine lurches forward, "You know somethin'—you're sick!" he shouts as his wheels bite into the ground. I stand and watch as he tears his way up the hill, mud flying off his wheels, stand and listen as the noise of his engine slowly fades around the bend.

Lincoln's father was right. When you can see the smoke from your neighbor's chimney, it's time to move.

SUNDAY EVENING: I'm an adult. Why am I bothered by such petty shit? I'm not. I have already written off the back road. Earlier I walked along it and, as I suspected, it was torn to pieces, Georgy's tracks having even rerouted the streams. A scarred and muddy mess. But it is half his road and this is America. Right? Furthermore, a man can only be hurt if he allows it. And I will not.

I marched the full length of the road and, sure enough, when I came to the back I found that the barricade marking the only joint Judeo-Vatican effort in the Goobersville area had been demolished. May a thousand drunks pass below Maud's window and terrify her until her heart stops and her eyes pop out of her head.

I took a deep breath and slowly exhaled. My breath came out in moonlit streams of smoke. The weather had suddenly become icy cold again. It was like a flood belatedly arriving after years of drought. The road was now turning hard and crunched under my feet. Slowly I strolled past our house and continued down toward the car—instinct or perhaps suspicion leading the way through a moonlit night cut by the shadows of naked trees.

Looking down from my vantage, I could see the Szorsky house, its cinder block base perched on a little prominence.

62

With the lights from its windows twinkling in the distance and reflecting off patches of snow, it seemed so tranquil and benign. A thin haze swept over the moon and fine flakes of snow began to fall as I reached my car. And then I looked down. For an instant I did a double-take, as though deceived by the darkness. Hardly able to believe it, I ran my hand along the torn body of my car. The entire left side and fender were crushed in, headlight and all, precisely where the Szorsky boy had so eagerly charged past. Disgusted I stared back down at the Szorsky house and the scene no longer struck me as peaceful.

It is late night now and yet I still feel angry, too furious to sleep. I feel soiled and dirtied, feel invaded as one must after being robbed, knowing that a stranger has rummaged through one's most private belongings. Well it's over now. Try to forget it. Forgive and forget. Anyway, the car wasn't worth very much and what the hell is a fender or so, compared with the suffering my forefathers experienced at the hands of the Poles and Cossacks. O.K. So my family didn't come from Poland or Russia. Why get hung up in technicalities?

MONDAY: Did I say all was over? Why do I always think I will get away so lightly?

Georgy, who never seems to be in school these days, has decided to give us a new rock concert. Well, at least he isn't destroying anything. I will simply discipline myself to learn to appreciate such talented groups as "Fats Magoo and the Don'ts."

TUESDAY: What will it be today, I ask Viveca? Will it be more music? Or perhaps more tractor action? Will the horses return to their previous positions or will our road be sabotaged with triple-headed nails?

Discussing the Szorkys and trying to figure out what's going on in their heads has become a full-time occupation. We are still futilely looking for motives. Georgy is like his mother, wild and mercurial, tuned in to her every emotion—sharing a bedroom with Ma for fourteen years has not been for naught. Maud didn't have to send him up here on the tractor, we reason. Barely had she started squawking than he was already up on that machine, that self-righteous killer-instinct ignited. What is so troubling about Georgy is that he is, or at least was, by far the brightest and most promising of Maud's litter. I have watched him grow up over the last twelve years into the living proof of Maud's greatest failure. Raising him on a sparse mental diet, well-seasoned with hate and prejudice, she has finally perfected another sour apple, though, as far as Georgy is concerned, his life is rich with righteousness. Like Bernie Kaufman, there is no conflict. Or is there?

As a little boy in Catholic school, besides mastering the art of being an altar boy, Georgy learned how to read and write—and did it, as I recall, remarkably well. There seemed to glimmer the possibility that Georgy would break the Szorsky mold cast by a domineering father, now dead, and filled by his placid brother and vegetable-like sister. Rambunctious, inquisitive, and straining at Maud's controls, all systems seemed go. Yet once Georgy entered high school, progress abruptly ended. Suddenly Georgy became sullen and indifferent and angry. Whereas Maud used to try to rein him in, she now turned to buying him off with expensive gadgets and toys, satisfying his every mechanical whim, terrified that if she didn't placate him, her baby might one day up and leave her.

But why the change? Or was it inevitable, considering that Georgy had Maud for a mother and Irma and Henry for elders; was it destined to arrive with puberty as sure as pimples and wet dreams? The Szorskys certainly are unique. They absolutely never travel. (The farthest point they have ever visited together is Whamsattsville, fifty miles away; though once, right after WW II, Maud went to New York City and hated it.) They also never go to a movie. The idea

65

of eating out is absurd, especially since it's so easy to dash down to the supermarket and save *all* that money. It seems as though, aside from television and the church, Maud has systematically cut off any outside influences. Smug and certain, they have created a world unto themselves: "Szorskyville" says Perry, summing it up in a nutshell.

But these are all symptoms, argues Viveca, who has also been a twelve year student of life behind the Szorskian curtain. What may best account for Georgy's sporadic hostility is that—as we have discovered—the Szorskys as a family have no *inner* life. Aside from anger they never express any emotion, never talk to one another, never issue more than a grunt or fart. When the need arrives for Georgy to speak to someone, to talk out his wretchedness, there is no one there. And that is why, says Viveca, he assaults us. His loudspeakers are a plea for help. Which is all fine and dandy, except that I don't have the hankering to be a psychiatrist for a psychopath.

What the kid needs, explains Dr. N., is for him to get away from his family. Let him hitch-hike across the continent, let him get a job on the Alaskan pipeline, let him join the Marines and get his head blown off.

Once, when Georgy was lucid and responding, I hinted that he ought to consider traveling for a while after high school.

"Where to?"

"Anywhere," I suggested.

"Why?"

"Why? Well, just to get some new impressions. Take a trip to California when you graduate."

"I don't like it there."

"How do you know? You've never been there."

"I've seen it on television."

"Then go to New York."

"It smells there. Too many cars."

"Did you smell it on television too?"

66

"Travel. That's all you think about. Travel here. Travel there. I like it here."

Which is fine, except he is doomed, in the clutches of mother Maud, to grow up to be another ball-less Henry.

The real enigma, Viveca and I repeatedly ponder, is why the children continue to live with their mother who is a noisy, vile virago, forever screeching and complaining. Why, when the rest of their generation is expressing vitriolic hatred toward their benign and generally kind parents, do these offspring cling to Mama? And why, I weep, why do I have to waste my valuable time psyching out the Szorskys?

TUESDAY AFTERNOON: A letter to Maud:

Dear Maud,

I am writing this letter since it's easier for me to put my feelings on paper and there's also less chance of a misunderstanding.

What has happened between us over the last few days seems so terribly unnecessary. I fully well realize that you own half the road. But I also hope that you realize that *I'm* the one who is forced to maintain it—by hand and with back-breaking labor. Leaving the horses on the road for close to two weeks in the same spot had destroyed much of my work, making it almost impossible to drive to our house.

Frankly, I find it very hard to understand how one minute you can be exceedingly friendly and the next minute turn on us. Our feelings, as you well know, have been very consistent toward you and your family. Over the years we have lived as good neighbors, cooperated and shown consideration for one another. This latest series of events seems to undo all that goodwill.

Sunday afternoon, after asking you to move the horses and getting no reply, I *carefully* (and with great risk to myself) moved your horses. For that I have been repaid with a damaged back road, a smashed in fender, and a day of unending noise.

I consider our friendship worth far more than the price of a fender, and therefore, I am willing to forget it all if only you'll take into consideration our need to keep the road in usable condition.

As you have often said, neighbors ought to be neighborly. And I well agree.

Please, let's call an end to this and return to our old ways.

Yours,

Neil

TUESDAY EVENING: I drive down and meet Maud returning from her drill press. As she emerges with Irma from her glistening Duster I advance on her with my letter.

"What's that?" she says, eyeing me suspiciously.

"It's a letter. Read it, think about it, then give me a call."

"You had no right to move our horses."

"Did I hurt them? Did I?"

Maud smiles through her frown. Irma-the-zucchini gives a little dumb grin.

"I just want to—"

"They ain't your property and—"

"Do you think I like moving horses? They almost killed me!" I exaggerate. Irma is smiling. Either she thinks it's funny or she wants to see me dead. Which is it? At least the feelings are consistent.

"I just want to show you one thing," I say, leading Maud by the hand— in her other claw is my letter. The only mail she ever gets is the union newsletter. "Look," I say, motioning to the crumpled fender.

"Who did that?"

"Georgy, in his eargerness to tear up the back road and open the drunk blockade."

"You sure?" she says, examining the crushed side with great interest.

TUESDAY NIGHT: "What am I going to do with that

68

boy?" Maud is confiding on the phone, all friendly, her feelings once again consistent, all that goodwill re-established. "I don't know what sometimes gets into him."

"He's bored."

"I work all day long at that factory. Get home so dog-tired. They changed my seniority. Moved me down. Union doesn't even give a damn. Had a headache. My back's been killing me again. Stand all day. Nobody does any housework around here but me. Laid off another ten people. Those teenagers in the shop—boy, are they a bunch of snotnoses these days."

One hour later we are all great friends. Maud and I have reached our understanding. Our understanding is this: They will piss on us, continue to wreck the land, create noise and destruction. And for that we will be consistent Christians, turning the other cheek of our ass for another kick. Well, at least it's all over. Whew.

WEDNESDAY: All over? It may be over with horses, (horses? That seems like ancient history now. Is that how this all got started?) but today we've got shooting trouble.

For the last hour, Georgy has been sitting on his stoop shooting at a can. Which is fine except that Georgy, his purported target and the road just below our house form a straight line. We are pinned down. He has been firing at a steady rate—already a good hundred rounds—and it sounds like a large caliber gun. Viveca wants to go down and meet the kids at the school bus, but doesn't dare make a run for it. If we rush past and get hit, it most certainly will be our fault for getting caught in the line of fire.

I think I am slowly beginning to understand, on a gut level, the unending conflict in the Mideast. There are certain disputes, especially those involving territorial infringement, that can be resolved only by violence.

Are my options rapidly being shrunk? Do I now have to raid the guerilla camp down the road and kill the leader? For every aggressive action initiated by the enemy must

69

there be a retaliatory strike? Is the next step my children getting maimed? And why, I ask the powers that lurk in the woods, why is it that all those grisly mass slayings of farm families always have to occur in such far off places as Kansas? Oh, Perry Smith and Dick Hickock, where are you today?

Anxiously Viveca watches the clock. Five minutes before the bus is scheduled to arrive, just before I decide to crawl on my belly past the firing line, there is a ceasefire. Viveca dashes down to the bus.

Noise. Shooting. Damaged road and rammed-in car. This is it, Georgy baby. O.K. for you, Charlie. I jump in my car and head for the Sheriff's office, the warrant they got out for me be damned. As we used to say in Brooklyn: enough is enough.

From behind the desk, the Sheriff's deputy greets me and smiles recognition. For an instant I panic. Fortunately, it's not the same poor slob who stumbled up the hill to serve my warrant. I'm edgy because in Goobersville there is no chance for anonymity. They know it every time you take a piss. For example, yesterday I had the misfortune of being by the mailbox just as the postman came around:

"Electric bill," said Elmo, leaning out of his jeep window and handing me an envelope. "Another bill from the dentist," he noted, examining the letter before passing it on. "Ward's catalog. What do you know—already the spring sale," said my mailman, dying to talk. "Oh. Almost forgot. Here's another letter from your mother. Why don't you ever write her?"

Say the secret word and divide a hundred dollars. I whisper it to the deputy and, immediately, I'm shown into the office of the chief of detectives. The secret word is "Szorsky." Thanks to numerous complaints from myself and the "witch down the road" they already have a whole Szorsky dossier. Apparently I am also something of a celebrity.

"You know, you're one very lucky man, Mr. Nudelman," says Detective Risputantini who just ditched his wife to take up with bosomy, seventeen-year-old Gladys Depuy (lack of anonymity can be a two-way street). "As I understand it, we had an arrest warrant out for you."

"Oh? Really?" I flush and try to feign surprise.

"Looks like this guy Gunz who signed the complaint just up and died," he grins.

"Oh. Yes. Gunz," I begin to mutter, sputtering some polite words about the unexpected and tragic passing of Professor Gunz as it suddenly begins to dawn on me that now, for the first time since coming to Goobersville, I am on the "right" side in the perpetual town-gown hostilities.

"Now, what can we do for you?" Detective R. asks as he cleans the dirt out from under his fingernails with the sharp edge of his handcuffs.

I explain my quandary, bringing him up to date on the Szorsky problem.

"Well, just fill out an information and we'll have the boy arrested," says Officer Risputantini, brightening noticeably. "Too bad you didn't come right in when he smashed your car. Shouldn't let things like that go too long. Now the harassment charge shouldn't be too hard . . . though attempted murder is a tougher charge to make stick. Haven't had one of those in ages," he says dreamily and I begin to wonder if I am hearing all this. Maybe Georgy was right? Maybe I should *move*? Maybe he was really trying to do me a favor? Maybe that benevolent and all-seeing God, whom the Szorskys worship so regularly each Sunday, was using Georgy as a conduit to beam me a message? Get out of Goobersville while you're still sane and/or alive.

"Anything short of arrest?"

"Not really."

"What the boy is really asking for is attention. Very frankly I suspect he may need psychiatric help."

"If he's arrested and convicted, the courts can impose

mandatory psychiatric treatment as part of a deal," says the officer, still keen on arrest in any form.

"But I don't want him arrested!"

"Look at it this way, if he's really sick you'll be doing him a favor."

"And what about myself? If I have that boy arrested and put under observation, I can kiss my road goodbye."

"You do have a valid point there," he says thoughtfully. "Why don't you bring charges against all of them?"

WEDNESDAY NIGHT: Chief Detective Risputantini does have a point there—I mean besides the one he is putting to Gladys. Arrest Georgy. Let him rot in the Goobersville hoosegow. Given the dangerous circumstances, I have no choice. I have made a firm and wise decision: one more thing, one more irritant and I'm throwing caution to the wind . . . Oh-oh . . . I think I hear music.

WEDNESDAY LATE NIGHT (or is it early morning?): The music's been going all night. This is it, folks. The final straw. Tomorrow morning I'm going right back to Chief Risputantini and together we will throw the book at Georgy . . . Now that I've made the decision I feel good, relieved, elated! Hahaha. To see that little fucker squirming behind bars. Such ecstasy. Maybe he'll be so depressed he'll hang himself before he's even arraigned.

THURSDAY MORNING: The music went all night. It's still going. Mixed fare. Rock & Roll. Country Western. Strange though, even lots of talk. But something's amiss. The music's not coming from the right direction. Where is it coming from?

I get dressed and go in search of the music. Finally I detect the source. Apparently after arriving home from the Sheriff's yesterday, in my agitated state I absently left my car radio running. It's been on all night. My battery is nearly dead. George Szorsky's going to pay for this.

THURSDAY AFTERNOON: Not a sound. Not a peep.

Georgy has been home from school for two hours already. Why doesn't he start something?

THURSDAY NIGHT: Nothing. Still absolutely nothing.

FRIDAY MORNING: The silence is making me nervous. Maybe he's building something with which to destroy us? Maybe he's simply gathering energy before the final onslaught? Georgy's silence is more unnerving than his behavior. Where, in all of this, fits Bernie Kaufman? To cover my ass I called Bernie and got a little carried away. I told him things were going even faster than I expected.

FRIDAY AFTERNOON: Georgy Szorsky is coming up the road to my house. He is walking on his two rear feet. No tractor. No minibike. He is carrying neither a gun nor portable hi-fi amplifier. And . . . on his face he is sporting a congenial, humane smile.

I hear his leaden feet ascending the wooden stairs leading up to my house. I run and hide in my room. I can't bear to see his face. Peeking through a crack in the bedroom door, I watch, utterly astounded, as Georgy amiably greets Viveca.

"Hi," chirps Georgy, "Do you still want me to fix up that cabinet?"

SATURDAY: Now, can you figure it out? As violently as his outburst started, it has subsided. This morning Georgy is in the kitchen rebuilding a cabinet for us, whistling and acting like a normal happy seventeen-year-old. It's as if he had read my mind and realized that I was not going to tolerate another transgression. The antennae which are tuned to his mother are also tuned to the outside world. Having finally succeeded in destroying my peace, threatening my sanity, and sucking me into his life, having left me with but shaking hands to attack Bernie's masterpiece, Georgy is now in bliss. What kind of finish would I like on the cabinet? he wants to know. Would I like him to get me one of those new, fancy types of handles? He has an extra pair down in his shop and could give it to me for nothing. For nothing?

73

Today marks exactly two weeks since the end of Georgy's seizure. In the interim I have managed to submit five revised chapters to Bernie—which may explain why Mr. Z. is now calling me urgently from New York, a bit in a tizzy.

"How, how could you do it?" asks Mr. Z. and I can almost hear him pulling his hair.

"I didn't plan it that way," I apologize meekly.

"Mr. Kaufman just called me—he was, to say the least, agitated. What he gave you was a serious book dealing with the private lives of businessmen and what have you done? You've gone and turned it into a farce!"

"Look, I didn't really intend to change his book, but novels and characters have a life all their own. Bernie's book, it appears, was a comedy, a natural comedy. I just brought out some of the hidden tones, that's all."

"Mr. Kaufman was livid. Said you were trying to make a fool out of him."

"Nothing of the kind, Mr. Z. I tried to write it straight, really, I swear, but it just turned around by itself—though professionally I think I'm doing him a big favor."

"I did remind him that you were one of the best, that you were on the verge of fame. I even told him about your last book *Paradise Regurgitated*. I think he was very impressed."

"Maybe I should go and see him."

"Yes. Yes," says Mr. Z. a bit relieved. "I think that'd be very advisable before you go much further. After all, I did recommend you and, well—"

"I know. I know. And I'm infinitely indebted. Honestly I am. I'll go see him," I promise, wondering just what it is I will say to Bernie and dreading the meeting.

No sooner do I put down the phone than it rings again. A

very busy day. It's Mandel calling to schmooze. He's sitting in his laboratory bored to tears, chewing his nails and wondering if the NSF is going to renew his grant for studying the life of an ionized helium atom in a magnetic field. This grant business is no small potatoes. If he doesn't get it the kids might not even be able to go to weight-watchers' camp.

"You know, Nudelman, you may have a little financial trouble, but your life isn't really that bad."

"Who's complaining?"

"Boy, funds are lean this year."

"Yup. Lean as a bean."

"Oh, apropos finances, there's a rumor going around town about you."

"About me? Another one?"

"I thought you'd enjoy it."

"Shoot."

"Spellman in linguistics came up to me today and said, 'Did you know, Nudelman comes from a very, very wealthy family?' "

Mandel laughs.

I laugh.

"It isn't true, is it?" he double checks, just in case.

Later, sitting and staring blankly at Chapter Seven of "Hearts and Hymens" I find my mind returning to Mandel's intercepted rumor. It's strange because my father was subject to the very same type of thing.

Fleeing from Vienna in 1938, Dad managed to leave behind not only the Nazis, but also a profitable law practice. Anything but a businessman, my father was soon to discover that eking out a living as a printer was at best touch and go, that the competition was fierce, and that, even if he did manage to land orders and deliver the finished job, there was no guarantee the merchandise would be accepted, much less paid for. He put in twelve hour days riding the subways and pounding the Manhattan pavement in search of those elusive "orders," sometimes with nothing to show. Yet in Kew Gardens, where I grew up, there was a persistent rumor—that tall, silver-haired Herr Doktor Nudelman was really a wealthy man.

Good old stoical Dad. Although it was the pursuit of money that held him prisoner of the subways and drove him to the point where he knew every crack in the pavement within miles of his shop on West Twenty-sixth Street, he just never learned to worship the almighty buck. Although he literally sweated and slaved to get it for us ungrateful little wretches, he also considered it utterly poor taste to talk about his income or lack of it. He never bargained, paid every bill regardless how ludicrous, and never, ever discussed the price of cars or a slice of meat. This odd behavior, coupled with his regal, old world appearance, could only be interpreted as a sign of sure wealth. Perhaps unconsciously, I've been following in his footsteps, shunning talk of money because I'm too embarrassed about my own financial failure, too ashamed of my selfish disregard for the state of my own family?

In any event, while the true well-to-dos, such as the Mandels, who've just recently inherited a second fortune, pass their idle moments recounting the bargains of yore, ne'er does a mention of *Geld* escape my lips.

Money. Money. Money. I continue to stare idly at Bernie's Chapter Seven. It's such an utter bore I could scream. In its bare bones, this chapter relates Peter Miller's first exciting day in London. Upon arrival, Pete checks into a plush hotel and then, without a wasted moment, calls the desk to arrange for some "unique entertainment"—not one, but (get this!) two live girls. For twenty-two pages, Pete Miller will line them up, position them, eat one pussy while fingering the other, while one of the girls is nibbling on his earlobe. Which might even be vaguely interesting, if Brother Kaufman didn't have the habit of repeating certain key phrases. After he fucks some bird, he always ends up remarking that, "It was better than ever before in his life." Or, "In his whole life, Pete Miller had never experienced a woman like Darlene." Or, "Never would he forget the body of Charlotte, it was better than he had ever before . . ." Or, "Never in his whole life had he ever. . ." Pfew! Feech!

Quickly I set to work revamping Chapter Seven. I skim through his pages, pick out the characters and their descriptions and then I'm off, my typewriter going a mile a minute, smoke issuing from the keyboard.

As I delve deeper and deeper into the newly progressing scene, I find myself first smirking, then giggling, then howling aloud. An hour later, drenched in sweat and holding my belly in pain from prolonged laughter, I'm finished. With just a little sleight of hand I have created ART: Pete Miller checks in, calls down to the front desk and, after five minutes, a girl arrives. "But I asked for *two*, you idiot!" he curtly snaps at the polite British desk clerk. Moments later, there's a knock on the door and Pete, hastily covering his genitals, eagerly opens up for girl number two. Moments later, and barely enough time to get into the swing of things, there's another knock and a third girl at the door who insists upon entering, entertaining and being paid. A little confused, Pete lets her in. From then on, every minute on the nose another chick arrives, forces her way in, strips and joins the crowd. New girls continue to arrive at an unprecedented rate, until the London streets are bare of women and those in Mr. Miller's suite are forced to climb over each other to make room for the next naked sardine who wedges herself in the door asking, "I say, is this Mr. Miller's room?" It is the desk clerk's Marx Brothers revenge for Pete's rudeness. As Chapter Seven closes, Bernie Kaufman, alias Pete Miller, is aswarm in limbs and titties with someone's beaver clamped over his face like a gas mask and there's another knock on the door. As I said, ART, pure ART.

Report #2 From The Group

Mr. Nudelman's is certainly not our only case, though following his actions has usurped more than a fair share of our limited time and energies. So much has happened since our last report that we are going to have to limit ourselves to a somewhat superficial analysis. The Group wishes to apologize for the omission of any events necessitated by a succinct report, and hopes that the reader will try to understand the tremendous pressure of growing case loads under which we are forced to operate.

As even the casual observer has ascertained, it would certainly not be difficult to convince any jury of Mr. Nudelman's peers that the subject is in a very critical and "crazy" phase—the hardest task might be to find such an assemblage of peers (and that is not meant to be facetious).

Given a job well within his capabilities, Nudelman has already begun to play havoc with his employer's intentions. Mr. Kaufman, a highly respected member of the business community, was generous enough to extend a helping hand to Mr. N., offering him a tasty German lunch in the bargain, only to discover that very hand bitten off above the elbow as Mr. N. ruthlessly proceeded to "bargain" this gentleman up from a prearranged payment of two dollars per page. Time and again, instead of being grateful, Mr. N. turns greedy. Is there no limit to his insatiable appetite?

Although he claims to have been writing for well over fifteen years, our subject has obviously failed to come to grips with an essential feature of his chosen profession: an

78

author writes for an audience. Historically, erotic novels descend from a time-honored and esteemed literary tradition stretching from Boccaccio to Rabelais to Jacqueline Susann. Whereas Mr. Kaufman, by his literary efforts, serves a well-defined audience, Mr. Nudelman appears to write in a void. Given the choice, what will readers opt for—Mr. Nudelman's relentless diatribes against society, or Mr. Kaufman's fast-moving narratives?

Instead of eagerly accepting this most promising opportunity which—as even Mr. N. realized—might easily lead to a lucrative career, he has subverted his employment by turning a serious, though perhaps amateurish, work into vulgar, slap-stick comedy. Worse, though more enlightening for our examination of his fundamental behavior patterns, we find that he is repeatedly using his "free hand" to make fun of the procreative act. It is just as the Szorsky boy so astutely commented as he drove past that eventful day on his tractor, "You know something," he remarked compassionately to Mr. N, "You're sick!"

As long as we are on the subject of the neighboring Szorskys, let us go back and examine in some brief detail this latest series of incidents.

Mr. N.'s complaints that young George Szorsky was disturbing him and thus preventing him from working on the Kaufman manuscript are interpreted by this group as stumbling blocks, conveniently erected by Mr. N., between himself and his typewriter. One can't help but yield to the temptation to compare his plight to that of the hyperkinetic child who, given the mildest distraction, eagerly seizes any pretext to stop working. With a span of concentration of little more than a half hour, with proverbial ants in his pants, how—we ask—will Mr. N. ever hold a job? It is a fundamental question that even his own children are beginning to ask. Sick. Sick. Sick. Do we need more evidence?

We in the Group have bent over backwards, as we often

do for our potential patients, combing in detail the latest series of events in Mr. N's life, but our ultimate findings militate against the prospects of our granting Mr. N. anything even vaguely approaching a clean bill of health. In summary form, let us briefly recapitulate some of the salient facts that led to our decision.

a) Re. Master G. Szorsky damaging Mr. N.'s car: *Examination of the car by our insurance specialist shows that there actually was concrete (as opposed to imaginary) damage. Our specialist does, however, also assure us that the injury was unintentional. "G.S.," reads his official findings, "was simply trying to get around the car and slipped sideways. Accidents will happen even to the best of us."*

b) Re. the music of G.S.: *Rock music is a recognized phenomenon of our time, much as Christians being thrown to lions was, for example, an ordinary event in ancient Rome. Just as, in this latter case, the victims were introduced into the arena solely to provide entertainment for the populace rather than pain for the Christians, so, too, loudness must be seen as a prerequisite for the appreciation of modern music, rather than as a malicious means of destroying other people's peace of mind.*

George Szorsky, as our investigation reveals, was just listening to his music outside his home, employing presently acceptable levels. In "no way," insists Mr. Szorsky in his deposition, was the music intended as a provocation. Rather, he was just "trying to feel the beat."

c) Re. the purported strafing and shooting: *This country has a long and time-honored tradition stressing self-defense and marksmanship, and young Szorsky was simply honing his skills with a firearm. With George Szorsky such a fine shot, the chances of a bullet missing the tin can and traveling on to the Nudelmans' road were, indeed, very remote.*

d) Re. the horses parked on the N. access road: *This*

initial item which precipitated a paranoic state (ultimately leading up to the point where N. blames G.S. for being in some way responsible for Nudelman leaving on his own car radio) could easily have been averted if the road had been graveled and asphalted according to parking lot specification.

As a final note on the Szorsky matter, it is not without a sense of accomplishment that we find our initial suspicions (report #1) of Mr. N.'s imagined sense of persecution (his identification with subjugated Negroes) borne out by his now, "understanding the Mideast conflict." In this most recent of neighborly misunderstandings, distortion by the subject has yielded the following equations: Mr. N. is the peace-loving and beleaguered State of Israel, and the Szorskys are the Palestinian terrorists. Mr. N. is the defenseless shtetl Jew and the S.s are the Cossacks initiating a new pogrom. Ingenious metaphorizing, perhaps, but the subject's assessment of his situation—in addition to being completely fabricated—is fraught with contradictions. No sooner has Mr. N. berated the Szorskys for their alleged prejudice and intolerance, than he, himself, stoops to denigrating their Polish-American heritage, ridiculing their Catholicism, blaspheming their minister and patronizing their regularity of worship. And what is the next step? Is it to curse our Lord Himself? If Mr. Nudelman does not accept the beliefs of other mortal and intelligent men, we in the Group can not help but ask, "What, Mr. Nudelman, just what exactly is it that you do believe in?"

During one of his frequent communications with this group Mr. Nudelman indicated that he was planning on beginning a new book, apparently to be entitled "Goobersville Breakdown." At the time of that communication, and on numerous subsequent occasions, we have unequivocally indicated that we deem it highly ill-advised. This purportedly biographical work in which he intends "to tell all" can have no salutary effects whatsoever

81

and can only result in his viciously slandering friends and neighbors, in rubbing open old and dangerous wounds.

Refusing to heed our warnings, it appears that he has, in fact, begun such a work and that he even intends to include a select number of our own reports in his "book"—that he is going to "spy" on us as a means of "paying us back" for our compassionate surveillance.

Since this is a free and democratic country and his actions to date have been, for the most part, vaguely legal, we have no means at our immediate disposal to prevent this dangerous course of action. That Mr. N. will ultimately bring upon himself the breakdown incorporated in his title goes without saying, but why must he persist in referring to the town he lives in as "Goobersville" when—as we all know—it has such a lovely name?

<u>Prognosis</u>: *Sick. Sick. Sick.*

For two hours now I have been standing motionless, planted in shin-deep snow like a naked telephone pole, stoically enduring a blinding blizzard just outside Roscoe, New York, frozen thumb extended into the breeze. The wind is so intense, blowing up swirls of drifting white, that I suspect the chances of a passing car spotting me, much less my beseeching finger, are close to nil. I am also beginning to seriously question the wisdom of this trip. Allegedly, I am on my way to the city to see Brother Bernie, though it is with a rising and ominous sense of dread that I have pursued this journey. The prospect of confronting Mr. Kaufman face-to-face, tête-à-tête, eye-to-eye, man-to-mouse, is little short of terrifying. Tucked away in the false security of my warm nest back in Goobersville, playfully doctoring up "Hearts and Hymens" may have been a big lark, but now I'm going to have to face the music and there is nothing I can say to Mr. Kaufman, no reasonable excuse to offer, no song to sing. I'm afraid this time the Group was right— though I'll be damned if I'll admit it to them.

Ah! The hell with Bernie. My real regret is that I have undoubtedly lost that precious income—money mentally spent three times over. Would it go for kids' clothes or a new muffler for the car? Should we stock the freezer in preparation for still leaner times? Do we buy shingles for the roof and replace the rotting board on the steps? Or should we just blow the whole wad on a trip to the sunny Caribbean and worry about the dire consequences when they arise? Needless to say, at this bleak moment, given the

choice between a new muffler and tires for the old crate or
building castles in the sun-warmed sand, I would opt for the
car repairs—someone in this country has to take seriously
the responsibility for stimulating a flagging auto-parts
industry.

Yes. Bernie's two bucks a page. Kept us going. The
yummy anticipation of his money had brought renewed joy
to our apathetic Appalachian lives, smiles to the smudge-
stained faces of my little urchins. Once again our family had
been brought together. Where formerly there had been
abject apathy, there was now a prayer. Why even the little
brats were taking part in our lively debates, injecting into
them their ignorant two cents' worth on how we should
spend *my* money. Look Bernie, look how happy you made
us with just the promise of but little more than what you
might spend for a night's orgasm. So why are you taking it
away? Don't you have any moral compunctions at all? And
when was the last time you were in a synagogue? Were you
dragged there out of obligation, reluctantly attending some
little pimpled fat boy's Bar Mitzvah? Or did you attend for
real, on your own firm convictions—like Maud and those
other God-fearing Goobersville souls who trudge so
devotedly each Sabbath to their house of worship?

Bernie, why are you doing this to us? To me? Why are you
such a stingy, miserable—No! You're right. The Group was
right. It's *all* my fault. I brought it down on myself. Oh,
what am I going to do? Bernie. Mr. Kaufman, sir. Please. In
the name of all you hold sacred and holy, please give me
another chance. Pretty please. I promise. I swear on my
mother's grave that this time I'll do it straight. No more
hanky-panky. No jokes. The rewrite I sent you was just a
test, to see if you had a sense of humor. Haha. And you *did!*
A wonderful, highly developed sense of humor. You proved
youself a better man than I, Gunga Din. A man like you,
Mr. Kaufman—I say, jabbering to myself as I flap my arms
like a penguin trying to keep warm—a man like you is one

in a million. A gem in the rough, that's you. Look at me, Mr. Kaufman. I'll hitch all the way to New York on my knees, if you'll just give me another try. One lousy chance. Is that so much?

Oh, what a mess! I mumble, getting up off the ground and brushing off my pants. Hardly have I begun and already this trip has been fraught with calamity—my misfortunes, I suspect, being little forewarnings of bigger disasters still patiently awaiting me. Why did I ever leave Goobersville? A better question: Why was I ever born? Very funny, I laugh, jumping up and down while wiggling my frostbitten ears, but when I was born to my *real* mother I actually tried to crawl back into her womb. With God and two astounded obstetricians as my witness. They never saw anything like it. I must have been a very perceptive fetus. Since that reluctant point it's been all downhill.

Oh, what a mess! My first hitch three hours ago turned out to be an elderly gent, tipsy to the gills.

"Why don't you let, errr . . . me drive," I suggested, holding on to the dash with white knuckles as we took off, weaving back and forth across the slick highway.

"Naw. Makes me nervous when someone else drives," the old bird muttered as the road took a turn and we continued straight, our car missing the highway, yet miraculously picking it up a few hundred feet later—the old coot driving on, cool as an orange popsicle.

"But I'm a very good driver," implored yours truly, trying to catch his breath. "I'm even a driving teacher. Hey, you wanna see my credentials. Ooops—Listen, I've taught some of the best. Even used to instruct Greyhound drivers."

"Naw. And stop distracting me," he grumbled angrily, discovering another car heading straight at him in what he began to insist was *his* lane.

Hopeless. Ill-fated. I fastened my seat belt and, closing my eyes, tried to mentally prepare myself for the inevitable: a few broken ribs and maybe even a dislocated shoulder thrown in for laughs. Or how about a collapsed lung, multiple leg fractures and a few severed tendons just to make it look good? I could sue the old fart for a fortune. Already I was visualizing myself on that lush tropical island, rolled out each morning to the beach in my wheel chair, motioning to the kids with a pencil in my mouth as I turn to busily completing my Goobersville memoirs.

To make a long story short, we barely made it to a point ten miles the other side of beautiful Binghamton—my inebriated friend careening off the road and into a ditch, performing an impressive double flip before rolling over again to come to rest on the roof. And as my usual luck would have it, I never was to get the chance to sue him, managing to sustain only minor damages resulting from the embarrassment of a little dribble of pee in my pants—hardly worth even taking to small claims court and definitely poor consolation, considering the enormous stakes that might have been realized.

And the second lift? That one proved considerably less dramatic, though equally trying—a balding man with silk shirt and blond toupé. From Utica he was, a traveling salesman for high pressure fittings, a gentleman—it quickly became evident—of the homosexual persuasion who, understandably, found me irresistible. I began by keeping up a constant patter of intellectually stimulating conversation, talking as much as humanly possible, producing a veritable mudslide of the American tongue. But by the time we reached Roscoe, I had already run out of extraordinary observations on the local flora and fauna and was beginning to repeat myself, when I looked down to discover his hand inching up my leg. Like a tarantula crawling up the inside of my thigh, it was hard to deny the existence of his hungry fingers. So I did what any sane man in my position would do—I told him the truth: that I really wanted to make it with him, here and now in this very car, this very instant, except that I thought I *might* still be contagious.

"Contagious?"

"I mean, if it doesn't bother you, I'm all game."

"Whatta you have?" he asked, scrutinizing me out of the corner of his eye as we danced over the icy road.

"I don't know what they call it, but every two weeks I've got to go to the hospital because my urethra grows together. And they've got to take this motorized instrument, it's like a Rotorooter and—."

Which brings me back here to Roscoe. And considering the fact that I have neither a place to stay in New York nor the desire to face up to Bernie, I'm getting to like Roscoe. Really. Got a charm of its own, it does. This place has gorgeous steep mountains loaded with emaciated deer, a fast moving stream by the road jumping with goose-pimpled trout, and the air is wonderfully damp. Who knows, maybe like General what's-his-face in the 1800's, I'll set up camp and stay here for the winter? To be utterly frank, this getting stranded is but water on a rat's ass. What really worries me is that a malevolent old gypsy once told my mother in Vienna or Cracow or wherever-it-was, that all bad things come in threes. And that has always struck me as a terribly cogent prophesy, one that has proven itself consistently true in my own life provided you count properly, starting with the right catastrophe.

Yes. Apropos my mother. Before leaving I called her in Palm Springs where she is presently occupied freeloading it off some generous millionaire. (Now *there's* a lady with the right idea!)

"Marry him," I cleverly suggest.

"Pfui! He's too *old*."

"But that's exactly the point, Mom. When he goes you'll be rich. Then, of course, we'll take care of you."

"I have my principles."

"I wish you'd adhere to them and marry him."

"What do you think I am?"

"My mother—or that's what you keep telling me."

"Are you joking?"

"Deadly serious. Listen, we could poison the old geezer. Does he have a favorite food like strawberry ice cream or Russian caviar?"

"I don't like your sense of humor."

"Look, the other reason I called—besides to tell you I love you—is that I have to go to New York for a couple of days on 'business' and I was wondering if I could use your apartment."

"Everything's closed up and packed away."

"But I won't need anything. Just a place to sleep. If I could borrow a couch—"

"Impossible. I just had them all reupholstered."

"The floor. I've got a sleeping bag."

"I left the place spic and span. Even the rugs were shampooed."

"I'm not going to make a mess."

"It took me hours just to get the floors waxed and—"

"What do you think I'm going to do, pee on the furniture?"

"If you make crumbs I'll have cockroaches *all over* when I get back," she shudders in disgust. "If you leave a window open the *burgulars* will come in. If you—"

"Look, I'll be very careful. I need a place to stay. I can't afford to pay thirty dollars a night for a hotel."

"Out of the question. Out of the question. When I'm there, fine, but I can't have you running in and out, sleeping on the floors like a hippie, making crumbs, leaving the lights on."

"I'll sleep on the bed. I won't eat in the house. I won't even use a light—I've got a flashlight. I'll lock the windows. I'll bark like a dog to keep criminals away. I'll dust your furniture with Pledge and wash your windows with Windex."

"Out of the question. And how are my little

89

grandchildren?" she asks, cheerfully switching the subject, as though I wouldn't notice.

So here I am, Mrs. N., somewhere in the Catskills, hopping up and down like a frozen kangaroo and waiting for horror number three, six, nine, or a multiple thereof to befall me. Under circumstances such as these it's hard not to curse one's mother. Not that I'm so sure she is. In the Bronx hospital where I was so reluctantly born, I was actually mixed up with an Irish baby. I was! Maybe I'm Irish? Maybe that's why Mrs. N. is treating me as she does. It's not that she's so worried about her fucking rugs, it's that she hates Micks. Acch! Curse that selfish, prejudiced woman! May the *burgulars* break into her god-damned Spic and Span apartment, leave on all the lights, and feed the cockroaches until they become the size of miniature Great Danes. Before entering her precious domicile, let them accidentally stumble into knee-deep heaps of dog turds and then do a jitterbug on her newly shampooed carpets. Let them crumble to smithereens her precious collection of little Viennese figurines and even—Pfui!—use the toilet without flushing. May these same heartless housebreakers be taken with the whim to use her phone to call their accomplices in Kuala Lumpur and Singapore person-to-person during the day rate, operator assisted. And above all, dear Lord, please be sure that when they finally do go they remember to leave open the windows to let in both the rain and all the other thieves who will eventually follow. Amen and thank you.

Which does absolutely nothing to solve my upcoming confrontation with Mr. Kaufman—though I have an idea, I do . . . Maybe, just maybe, I can turn this impending defeat with Bernie into a minor victory, milk a little pleasure out of torment . . . Perhaps I can arrange to meet Bernie over a little lunch to discuss the dismaying state of the rewrite. Maybe even drag it out to a little dinner afterwards at The Palace or say, Pierre Au Tunnel, to discuss his literary career in still greater depth. How does a little

90

midnight soupé of crêpes and wine sound, an intimate moment to jointly outline the plot of say, novel number twenty-three? And has he considered doing screenplays? Stage plays? Lyrics to pop songs or operas? Why with his talent the possibilities are limitless, the tasks but trifles, formalities at best. And while we're at it, how about a little side order of kosher bacon, maybe a hot fudge sundae with nuts and whipped cream for dessert? Between spoonfuls, I will keep up a scintillating conversation, a verbal dissertation spotted with literary allusions like the dark bitter nuggets in chocolate-chip ice cream, my favorite flavor. I am so utterly famished and taken up with Bernie's generosity that I fail to notice the passing car that slows down and then stops. It honks. Startled, I jump a little into the air and then charge off on feet which function like frozen stilts.

"Hi," I smile opening the door to suddenly discover a familiar face.

"Mr. Nudelman!" chirps this willowy blond thing.

"Miss . . . Errr . . . Miss. No, no. Let me guess," I say climbing into her sleek, warm sports car.

"Finite Math," she helps.

"Right! Tuesday, Thursday at three."

"For sure, for sure," she laughs pulling away, the car moving without effort and floating on springs of marshmallow.

"Miss Schmelk."

"Call me Stephie."

"O.K. *Stephie.* Call me Sam."

"I had you four years ago, *Sam.*"

"Never forget it."

"You were really a great teacher, really, some heavy mind."

"I've lost a little weight since then."

"And very hilarious, like wow."

"I'm sorry I had to fail you, honestly I am," I apologize to call-me-Stephie who, I fear, to this day still thinks a probability function is something like a bowel movement, a Markov Chain an item used to lock up a bicycle, and a permutation group a session in which one confronts one's deepest anxieties.

"Oh, I deserved it. Never had much of a head for math," says call-me-Stephie, dreamily winding her long tresses around her middle finger as she guides her power-steered machine through the white tornadoes. "If you'd like, there's some food back there."

"I'm not really hungry—in fact, I just had a huge dinner," I shrug, turning around just to check.

"Nothing very special," she calls out as I reconnoiter her picnic basket. "I think there's two egg salad on rye left."

"Well . . . I suppose I *could* manage maybe one—and perhaps something to wash it down with?"

"There's a thermos of coffee somewhere back there."

"Success. Just found it."

"The other sandwich'll go to waste if you don't—"

"Well, in *that* case," mumbles Professor N. with a full mouth, already three-quarters of the way through number one, ". . . what with world famine and drought, I think I'll take my responsibilities seriously and help you with the other sandwich, too," he smiles, egg salad on his lips, relishing those gulped morsels which noisily land in his hollow stomach like tennis balls dropped into a metal bucket.

"How far are you going?" I yawn a few minutes later, the warmth of her car and a full belly conspiring to make me deliciously drowsy as I go on to discover in her bottomless basket cupcakes with chocolate icing, brownies with walnuts, and a few lonely dill pickles—all in imminent danger of going to waste.

"New York City," she nods.

"Wonderful!" Aha, the gypsy was wrong. "Me too. Such a coincidence. I'm going down there to pick up my new car—

the one I just ordered. I was going to take the Greyhound, but I simply loathe sitting like a canned herring on a stuffy bus and being smoked to death. Give me the free and open life of the road," explains this former man of mathematics, a wee bit expansively, still a little high on mayonnaise. "You know, the *Easy Rider* thing, but without the motorcycle," continues the good professor before unexpectedly slipping off into sleep.

.   .   .

For the length of route 17, the New York Thruway and the Palisades Parkway, I have been having a nightmare, dreaming that Leif and Magnus—now both grown young men—have, despite my vehement warnings and urgent protestations, gone on to become a scientist and writer, respectively. Leif, it appears—in just his first year of graduate studies—has already discovered the cure for the common cold, while creatively-inclined Magnus, forsaking college, is churning out novels for unprecedented advances almost as fast as the publishers can write out the checks. Both boys—barely out of diapers and already at the pinnacle of achievement—are putting their father to shame in precisely his own fields of failure. And not only that! As though to add insult to injury, Viveca has discovered a revolutionary new way of preparing foods that sidesteps the entire process of cooking, while my Irish setter Pluto has suddenly—in his waning years—learned to talk, the dog scheduled to be interviewed shortly for the cover story in *Newsweek.* I am surrounded by unparalleled achievement, awards and other forms of recognition. And what am *I* doing? Through all this commotion I am *still* laboring on the first page of my *Goobersville Breakdown* memoirs, somehow unable to get the syntax right in the third paragraph.

93

"You should be proud," pleads Viveca, gently trying to prod me into magnanimity.

"Proud? How can I be proud, when I am jealous of Miss Schmelk who has never known hunger or anguish or despair—and never will!" I fume, suddenly waking up to find myself in Stephie Schmelk's car trapped in traffic at the approach to the George Washington Bridge—my kids, wife and hound all still undiscovered talents, while Stephie, unaware of my confused and groggy state, is bubbling away, telling me about her future. Her father, one of the most respected men in ladies' panties, she is explaining, has finally decided to let her take a whack at acting and being independent. No more *futzing* around with liberal arts for her, no sir. So, beginning this semester, she's renting an apartment in the city and enrolling in acting school, success but a sneeze away. And this is no fly-by-night decision, she informs her yawning, stretching audience—and that's why her Daddy's picking up the three hundred dollar tab on her new digs. Stephie—I am impressed to learn—has been pondering her career for a long time, in fact the whole fall semester, even going so far as to "develop" her mind.

"When you had me as a student I wasn't intellectually bent, but, like, things have changed. I'm finally getting my stuff together, doing a lot of reading. I think that an actress needs to have a reality of her own, a *Weltanschauung*."

"Selbstverständlich," I answer, trying to be my usual agreeable self, still pondering the meanings of my own dream, and not having the vaguest idea what she could be talking about.

"I've been getting into D. H. Lawrence."

"Really?" I ask, raising my eyebrows and wondering if in addition to being an intellectual, she is also a necrophile.

"Now that I'm finding out where his head is at, I really dig him."

"Was."

"Huh?"

94

"Was. He's dead," explains the old school teacher indulgently.

"Or was," she giggles and, obliviously enraptured in her own dream, proceeds to tell me how she's on a whole new trip, how because of *reading*, her life's one wild new bag.

"No kidding," I shake my head, thoroughly awed and utterly glad to be out of the teaching racket where every day I was exposed to the wisdom of a hundred other Stephies and their professorial mentors—students and teachers either too lazy or stupid to be able to think or speak English, picking up all those wonderful intellectual rags and meaningless doodads and dressing up in them as if they were furs and jewels. Or is it *me*? Does all this make sense? Have I been crippled by a scientific background which shuns the metaphysical and demands theorems and physical proof? Is it that which has left me so utterly intolerant of people who ask me if I was born under the sign of Aquarius or wish to help me purify my soul via transcendental meditation and lunar gravity?

"Whole new bag?" I echo, feeling distinctly uncomfortable, though straining to be polite, sensing myself drifting into the quicksands of imbecility.

"My lover's a woman," says Stephie, smiling a perfect set of orthodontured teeth, flashing that warm and vacant smile I used to face, three rows from the window, fifth seat down.

"Well, that makes two of us," I laugh, blown away. Freaky, that. Spacy. Spicy, too. What a pity. Such a waste. "Far out," I nod, weighing the revelation. "So you're a . . . a . . ."

"Oh no! I'm *bisexual*. That's my reality now."

"That so?"

"And not only that."

"Oh?"

"I'm also a vegetarian."

"Wow!" I smile and think to myself: who would *ever* have guessed, looking at this lovely young lady with shapely legs and peaches-and-cream complexion, straight teeth and perfect nose, that she is a vegetarian? Who? And as we drive off the George Washington Bridge onto the West Side Highway, I can't help but wonder what General George would have said to all this were he here today. Would he be able to pick up on it or would it blow his mind? Would he be laid back or uptight? Would he freak out or be able to get his shit together and relate to it? Could he hear where she's coming from or get real heavy and hard-assed?

No! I warn myself. Stop it! Don't make fun of her. Why spoil her joy, pop her pimple of pleasure? Is your life such a gas that you can afford to laugh at hers? Listen, she's not hurting anybody with her asinine idiocy. Why, if it gives her pleasure, I say let her pursue her wildest whims. If it gives her kicks, let her wear bouquets of broccoli behind her ears as she nibbles her girlfriend's pussy. Let her direct a choir of naked idiots, twiddling an asparagus stalk for a baton as they chant in rounds the opening three-and-a-half lines of *Sons and Lovers.* Let her play Lady Macbeth on the New York stage, clad only in a kimono stitched together from three-thousand-and-one dried cucumber skins. Nudelman, Nudelman, you filthy old drop-out, jaded and bored as you are, why must you burst this lovely bubble of youth, soil the dreams of this delicate Princess Schmelk? She has shown you nothing but kindness and mayonnaise, and for that you are going to repay her by making light of her intellectual development, laughing at her new-found bisexuality, and bruising the vulnerable fruits of her herbivorosity. Nudelman, you blood-thirsty carcass vulture, you are no better than the Nazis who forced your kosher forebearers to munch on the raw intestines of swine. Professor N., I must warn you: do as you did in those good old Goobersville U. days, when God was a regular weekly check minus Federal and State withholding tax. Bite your tongue, smile, be *pleasant* and above all try not to think. Remember, today's fool could be tomorrow's leader. For all you know Stephie may forsake bit acting for high drama and become President. This country's done worse. Who knows, the way things are going the Miss Schmelks of America may inherit the earth. And if not them, then perhaps the Szorskys. And what has all this got to do with my own survival? Little, except that I can't dismiss the crazy notion that maybe Stephie's father could get me a job in the undies racket.

Yeech. The trouble with being poor is not just the absence of money; it's this constant battle with bitterness— begrudging those that have. Why else am I mentally dumping on a basically kind Miss Schmelk? And why am I forever carrying on these insane conversations with myself, I am wondering as traffic suddenly thins. We are moving again and before me looms the impressive skyline of west Manhattan. My heart takes a pleasant little hop. "Manhattan," I say aloud, invoking those poor Algonquins who had absolutely no sense of real estate values, hurriedly listing their property at the first sign of whites only to fall prey to a sharpy like Peter Minhuit who—as Maud might say—Jewed 'em down to an old trunk of beads. Ah. When I hear the word *Manhattan,* I can't help but see the Dutch bowling on the greens of the Battery. Then too, I think of the English haunting the streets in powdered wigs, or the later boatloads of immigrants crowding into the tenements of the Lower East Side. All romantic horseshit, gleaned from third grade history books, no doubt, but it's still there in my mind. Hmmm, Manhattan. Already I am thinking of bakery windows overflowing with fresh fruit pastries, see those loaves of crisp-crusted rye or pumpernickel piled high on the shelves, spicy caraway seeds clinging to their skins, begging to be nipped off and popped in your mouth.

Coming into Manhattan from the Goobersville woods is always thrilling, a little charge to the old battery. And while others may only smell the rank pollutants and grime of millions of souls, I detect the whiff of food as sure as the nose on my face—Chinese and French and Pakistani and

97

Italian and Arabic; baklava and coq au vin and pork poi. Spicy curry and icy spumoni. Herrings that have been mercifully drowned in cool, smooth, white sour cream.

At this moment New York strikes yours truly as one big smorgasbord table, those seductive aromas fanning out like radio signals. And as we drive down the West Side I am dizzily zeroing in on all those luscious smells. Like a hungry hound that hasn't had more than a couple of pilfered egg salads in a week, I am floating above this strange island while Stephie is still holding forth on her idol, D. H. Lawrence, and all three of his books which she has studied in depth. While in my mind's eye I see Ellis Island and miles of refugees lining up at customs, see the big shots of old Tammany Hall in their vests and spats making sure the votes in their precincts get turned out, see the carriages of the wealthy pulled across the cobblestone streets of this city by high-stepping strutters, Stephie is explaining to me how her reality and D. H. Lawrence's have finally merged. Yes. Yes. Yes. Tell me more Stephie. Spare me nothing.

"Have you gotten into any of his books?" she asks, breaking into my reverie, quizzically tilting her head and questioning me with those innocent doe-like eyes that will take the New York theaters by storm.

"Lawrence?" I repeat, concentrating on the streets outside that glisten dark and wet like seams of coal. "Sex never really was my bag of tea," says our hero, trying to be amusing while struggling to figure out just where to go.

"Hey, where are you going?" asks Stephie, that perceptive mind reader, as we drive through the Fifties, the streets beginning to turn mushy white with the rush hour traffic gone.

"I thought I'd stay at the Hampshire House," says I not batting an eyelash. "You can just let me off here. I like walking through the city," I explain. And I do, really.

"I'd let you crash at my place, but it's, like, tiny. I don't think my lover would think it's too cool."

"Cool. Hot. Think nothing of it and listen, thanks loads for the lift," I bubble, pulling on my shabby coat that somehow seems suddenly shabbier as she stops at the curb. "You're a real angel," says I, blowing her an appreciative kiss. "And thanks for the cupcakes and sandwiches and brownies and coffee and pickles."

"Bye-bye," waves this sprightly underpants heiress as she drives off to her lover, D. H. Lawrence and a hearty diet of sliced carrot sticks.

"See you on Broadway, kiddo," I wave back, her car long since gone.

Finding suitable accommodations in New York is no mean task. I'd stay at the Americana, honestly I would, except that word has it that as of late the food is ghastly. The Plaza, it turns out, has been taken over by a new crowd of riffraff. As for the Carlisle, St. Regis or Pierre, they are simply out of the question. Finally, after an hour of meandering through the streets and checking out some of the lesser known establishments, many of which I discover have recently gone over to an hourly rate, I decide to opt for a good old reliable inn like the Eastside "Y".

Schlepping my satchel across town, I can't help but think back fondly on dear Mater. Before leaving town I just *must* buy a large box of Tip Top Breadcrumbs for all her little friends. Ah, dear meticulous woman, my old lady. She was so neat, I remember, that when my father would get up at night to go to the bathroom she'd jump up and make his bed. To this day, thanks to her tidiness, I still can't sit on a 'foreign' toilet seat without spreading a little doily, still can't use a fork in Horn & Hardart without first wiping it with a wet napkin.

Soak-footed and weary-skinned, I trudge across the island to the Y. The building is a massive and forbidding brick structure, austere and unwelcoming. Hesitating in front of the entrance, I look up at the endless rows of sooty windows gouged into the façade like pox scars on a lifeless face— stand there in the dripping snow, I do, undergoing a last minute debate. A little voice inside keeps nagging. Pass it by, it says. Sleep on a bench in Grand Central if you must,

100

but don't go in. And why the YMCA of all places? asks the voice. You are neither young, nor Christian, and your manhood is already seriously in question. But the price is right, I argue, and I'm too dogtired to play games with little voices that don't exist. Leave me alone. I need rest. I need peace. I need to gather my energies to face the next onslaught in which a hoard of one thousand yellow-skinned creditors will rush me with drawn bayonets.

Pulling open the front door, I first peek in and then gingerly enter the foyer. Oh-oh, the voice was right, I think, assailed by the utter sleaziness of the interior, by the walls which are a dreary peeling grey, by the stained and yellowed lampshades of the few remaining lamps that still have bulbs, by rugs worn threadbare and fouled with dirt, by the listless clientele who move through the halls in slow motion like drugged ants caught in honey.

Submitting to momentum, I proceed into the lobby. Here the air is greasy and rancid. It smells of stale cafeteria food, of cabbage and potatoes and reheated franks, of yesterday's grilled cheese and tomorrow's despair. For a long moment I stand with my bag at my feet, a little lost, unable to pull myself to the front desk, overcome with depression and teetering on the brink of tears—and for what? What the hell, I try to brave it, all you need is a place to crash, a pillow for your head. And since when, Nudelman, have you become so fussy? You who have willingly shared accommodations with bedbugs and lice in Dakar and Macao, you who—But that was in West Africa, in Asia, and *that* was exotic adventure! *This*? This is home. This is where I grew up. I am an authority on every cracked square of sidewalk, every back alley in all of the five boroughs. Home! I should be welcomed back like a returning victorious prince. I should be greeted by a warm house bright with lights and family, hailed by a brass band in white gloves, ushered into a vast hall containing a mile long smorgasbord. Like General MacArthur or the Astronauts, I should be cruising down Fifth Avenue in a ticker tape parade, not slinking through the side door of a grundgy Y. Nudelman, the lobby says to me in terms so cogent, Nudelman, you're on the skids for real.

Come on. Pull yourself together! Listen fella, don't be such a high-falutin' schmuck. There probably ain't a vermin or bedbug in the house. It's the Y. America. Guaranteed clean sheets, clean people—take your pick. Stop being so dramatic about a lousy bed. Think of all the great men who probably sacked out here at one time or another during leaner moments—Walt Rostow, Henry Kissinger, Ponce de Leon. Who knows, maybe even Dreiser and Fitzgerald. When you think about it, the possibilities are infinite. So think! Perhaps you'll even catch some great inspiration. The place is probably crawling with fresh material.

Ugh! Although my arguments all make wonderful sense, are logical, rational and clear, there is still something pregnantly depressing about this joint with its miasma of wretchedness that hangs heavy in the air, this palpable poison of violence that seems to fester below the skin like an infected boil. What an absolutely magnificent setting for self-destruction, I remark to myself, selecting, as I do, sites conducive to suicide much as a filmmaker might search out ideal locations.

With steel in my spine and water in my shoes, I glumly pick my way through the corpses in the lobby and reach the front desk. Behind the counter is a tired West Indian, the whites of his eyes so yellowed that I wish I could scrub them with Pepsodent.

"I'd like an inexpensive single. Nothing fancy. Just—"

Hardly have I begun my request than a team of police suddenly charges through the front door into the lobby, rushing past the desk. "What floor?" cries one of the cops as others nervously poke at the bank of buttons on the elevators.

"Fifteen," says the clerk motioning indifferently upward

102

through all the commotion as another pair of cops comes barreling through the lobby lugging a stretcher.

"I can give you de room fo tree-fifty," says the clerk turning back to me as though nothing had transpired.

"What's that all about?"

"Oh dat? Some guy done cut his wrists," he shrugs.

"Cut his wrists! But why?" I inanely ask, my heart beating wildly. So I was right!

"You want de room, mahn?"

The room. Yes. It's on the twentieth floor; a windowless closet, a cubbyhole equipped with steel bed and dirty blankets. Wet plaster is raining down in gobs from a leak in the ceiling. The heat is going full blast and can't be turned off. The air in the room tastes of old men and rancid semen, of cheap gin and cigarette smoke, of yearning, regret, failure, human misery and loneliness. But the sheets are clean. Maybe what I really need is a good hot shower and shave.

At the other end of the corridor, the bathroom is doing a brisk business. The air is filled with steam and the sound of rushing water. Though it is winter, the long windows stand wide open looking out on adjacent wings, the interior sections forming a dark shaft that plunges down twenty floors.

Longing to feel the pounding of hot water on my back, I slowly start to undress. Yet, as I begin to peel off layer after layer, I suddenly sense the weight of eyes watching the progress of my undress. I stop. At every second mirror along the line of twenty-odd washbasins there are dandies of every size, shape and color who, I suspect, have probably been standing there all afternoon combing their hair in patient expectation. There are whites and blacks, Asians and Indians, all eyes and all eagerly waiting to check out the shape and dimensions of my Schwanz.

"Don't leave your stuff there," says a passing old geezer in

103

baggy, yellowed, long underwear, his nose red and bulbous, eyes rheumy.

"Huh?" I turn distracted.

"Somebody'll swipe it. And take your key with you into the shower."

"Oh?"

"Sometimes they grab your key while you're in the shower, run into your room and empty it out before you know it."

"Thanks," I smile appreciatively. Sounds like a nice establishment. Should have brought the wife and kids and dog.

"Last week they tried to take a key from one guy, see, and he wouldn't give it up. Two niggers threw him out the window," he shrugs, motioning with his chin toward the long window I had just looked out of. Worriedly, I stare again at the opening in the wall which stretches nearly from floor to ceiling.

"If anybody'd want my key, I'd gladly give it to them," says I a bit loudly.

"Smartest thing," says the old man. "But don't worry," he smiles kindly.

"Who's worried?" I say, my voice rising a half octave.

"You look like you can take care of yourself," he says reassuringly. "And don't worry about them," he winks toward our audience. "They won't hurt you none. They just want to look."

.   .   .

It's after twelve, I think. Maybe later. I hear voices in the night. Men are shuffling up and down the corridor in front of my room. With the transom open for air, I see their shadows wandering across the ceiling of my windowless coffin. I want to sleep, need to sleep, but I can't. My body is exhausted from the trip, but my mind burns with nonsense and my stomach rumbles emptily. The radiator bangs and hisses. I toss and throw a pillow over my head and then rip it off. I crave sleep, but sleep is elusive. Nights which once were so sweet have become torture. Sleep is the enemy. Can't trust it. It exposes me to the demons and dybbuks.

Over and over again I hear the voices of my little boys repeating those same worn out riddles:

> Question: Why does Barbie have pink tits?
> Answer: Because G.I. Joe has Kung Fu grip.

> Question: What's black and white and red all over?
> Answer: A nun playing with razor blades.

Ha! Razor blades. Ask the man on the fifteenth floor. He'd tell you. I hear mumbling in the corridor. My watch says two A.M. Doesn't anybody sleep around here? I get up and pace the dark room, fiddle with the jammed radiator, hum a loud tune. I lie down again and then I am thinking of Viveca and the argument we had just before I left.

"Why the hell don't you go out and get a job? It's not fair putting all the responsibility on me," I ranted, caught in the old trap.

"I'll try, if that's what you want. I don't know if I can find any—"

"If you *want to* you *can!*"

"O.K. Fine! But that means you'd better take care of the kids and house and clean and—"

"I can't! I'm too busy as it is just repairing everything around here. This place is going to pieces. It's in shambles. I can't even buy materials. I just keep patching and patching. And I need time to write!"

"You're *not* writing at all!"

"But I *might.* And then if I wanted to I couldn't!"

"But I can't be in two places at once! What, just what is it that you want?"

"I want peace! I need peace!" I cried and tore at my hair

as if Viveca could grant it, poor girl that she is.

Viveca, oh Viveca. Why the hell did you ever marry such a madman? You should have stayed with K. He loved you so. He would have laid the world at your feet. Today you'd be an elegant lady, your closets would be bulging with gorgeous gowns, the latest fashions. You would have maids and governesses and gardeners, a townhouse in the city and a country villa by the river. And K. would have worshipped you, never tortured you as I have. Oh, if he could see us today he would murder me; kill me, not for stealing you, but for treating you as I do. Instead of presiding over exquisite dinners and soirées, you have buried yourself in the Goobersville woods with a lunatic who can no longer even tell you that he loves you. Instead of proclaiming his affections, he attacks you, then slinks away like the lowly worm he is.

Viveca, oh Viveca. I am writing this tonight for you and you alone. What has become of us? Where have those luscious days gone, those days when we used to laugh and be carefree, when we made love nonstop, when I gave you a baby just for the wild impulse of it?

Viveca, listen to me. Can you hear me in the woods? I want to stand on the top of this broken dresser, stand up here in this horrible flophouse and crow like a rooster that I love you madly. I want to stamp my feet, rip off my clothes, balance on a fingertip and pull crazy faces. I want to throw caution to the winds, burn money, dance on my toes. Listen to me, Viveca. I will rob a bank with you and then we'll run away to Afghanistan or Tibet or the Fijis. There, with bare hands, I will chop down whole forests and build you a mansion. We will consume vats of vintage wines and dance in each others' arms in wild circles until we are drunk and dizzy with delight. I will be with you again free of worry, of want, be with you to taste again the excitement of rediscovered lust; hold you and stroke you and make love with you until we are bathed in a delicious sweat. With my

hands I will explore every curve and fold of your frame. With my tongue I will caress every square centimeter of your silky body, kiss your eyes and tickle your toes.

Viveca, oh Viveca, why must love be so tortured? Why do we make demands on each other, chalk-lines to the heavens we can never follow? Why can't I be man enough to take you in my arms, angry as you are, and kiss away despair, instead of hopping off like an insensitive toad?

Viveca, oh Viveca, how is it possible that a man who was once so funny and carefree and happily crazy, could become so moody and dark? How is it possible that a man who has always lived for the moment and wild impulse, can learn to delay gratification, become logical and worldly and, worst of all, calculating.

Viveca. Listen to me. Can you hear me in that jungle outpost of ours amidst the towering pines and hip-deep snows as I call to you from my twentieth floor transmitting post? Viveca, I am sending urgent messages to Goobersville this cold night. Read me loud and clear and make no mistake about it. Even if you should run back to K., take off with him on a round-the-world expedition, I will still love you, forgive you and even carry your bags. It is not fidelity in bed I crave, but fidelity in the head. And if you know what's good for you, you *will* go back to K. He'll support you in style, make you into the princess that you are. If I know him, he'll even want the children, your children, want them and take them on an endless spree, buying them those Vertibirds, G.I. Joe desert action sets, and AFX slot racers they so hunger for. He will dine you all on Lobster Thermidor, Shrimp Scampi, Strawberry Shortcake filled with fresh strawberries and topped with billowing mounds of whipped cream. Who knows, maybe I can even sneak along and work as his gardener or chauffeur or butler? Given the chance and a meager wage, I will polish his car until it glistens with a blinding shine, plant miles of petunias and posies, rebuild his entire mansion, carry your burdens like a donkey. He can toss me leftovers like a dog and I will lick his hairy generous hand.

I lie back. Ah . . . I think I am finally beginning to doze . . . My eyes become heavy and slowly the shadows on the ceiling fade, the voices outside my room turn to murmurs . . . I am thinking of Arnold before he killed himself, gifted painter and dear friend that he was . . . I am recalling that letter he sent prior to that last visit he was never to make, when we still lived in that old canvas-topped trailer on our mountain without electricity or water or heat.

Baron Nudelman,
Expect to arrive Mt. Nudelman August 3. In all probability will be traveling with companion who has undergone serious psychic mutation. Excellent conversationalist who should provide the Baron with interesting evenings. Please prepare trailer for my arrival—fresh paint, hot water, electricity, etc. Be sure to eliminate all irregularities which might prove troublesome. Born and bred to penthouse living, I am very sensitive to the lack of modern convenience. Oh yes, make certain that the fields are properly prepared to accommodate my bathroom functions. Begin with digging the holes now and lining them with gold foil. I never like to be seen evacuating in the same spot twice. Also, be sure to have your finest china and silverware sparkling and ready— under no circumstance can we tolerate paper plates or plastic utensils.
Please have welcoming band stationed in readiness by the neighboring Szorsky estates, the satin sheets pressed and cooled, the trailer air-conditioned to about 68 degrees. Otherwise, no demands.
Arnold

Poor Arnold, I am still thinking, when suddenly my

109

thoughts are jolted by an unexpected sound—someone fiddling with the lock on my door. Thieves? Queers? Murderers? My strength trickling away and deserting me, I lie perfectly still in bed, listening, listening . . . Click.Click. Click. The room is nearly dark. Damn! Those bastards must have unscrewed the bulbs in the corridors. Sounds to me like he's picking the lock with a length of wire. Lying frozen in bed with my eyes riveted to the door, I feel my heart pound away in my chest, my head spins dizzily with fear. Do something! Do something! I rail at myself, but for some stupid reason I am completely helpless and immobile.

Click. Click. Click. He keeps poking away at the hole. Idiot! I curse myself. Why didn't you listen to your own instincts? How could you fall into a rat-trap like this? Grand Central or Port Authority or even a cruddy subway car would have been better, safer, people all around.

Click. Click. Silence. The lock cylinder rotates. A snap. In the near darkness I can see the doorknob turn. Then, the door to my room slowly eases open, moving as if the hinges were newly greased. Slowly. Slowly. First a cautious crack. A long pause. Then an inch. Another inch. God! What am I going to do?

Then suddenly I see him—the thief, assailant, sex-fiend, mugger—his silhouette framed in the doorway; an enormous burly man, so tall that his head almost touches the top of the passage, chest and shoulders so wide that his body plugs the doorway like a cork.

"What do you want?" I ask, feeling the last ounces of fight drain out of me as though I were punctured by a volley of machine gun bullets. No answer. Petrified, I watch him as he stands there, his eyes first sweeping my room before finally fastening on me, his body coiled like a predator ready to lunge.

"Get the fuck out of here!" I hiss loudly, hoping to intimidate him, praying that he won't detect the fear in my

110

voice. "Get out!" I yell, "or I'll break every bone in your body!"

Nothing. Not a ripple. He remains locked in that same poised position, his muscles flexed—his eyes fastened on me. What in God's name does this creep want? Why does he keep staring? Damn, I've got to do something. What? Anything!

"If you don't get out this instant I'll—Hey. Listen, you're asking for it! I know karate. I'm a black belt. Legally my hands are considered lethal weapons," I say holding them up like knives. "It's my duty to warn you," I growl with authority as this gorilla lurks in the shadows by the door. Then, suddenly, he begins to ease toward me, moving lightly on his toes like a dancer.

"O.K. buddy, you've been warned!" says I, sitting up in bed and assuming what I think is the right position for attack. "Bonzaaiii!" I yell, wildly waving my chops as, but inches away from my bed, he comes to an abrupt halt and looking down at my terrified figure, begins to smile, the weirdest twisted smile I have ever seen—a gold tooth flashing for an instant between his lips. Instinctively I gasp, preparing myself for the inevitable blow that will ram me into oblivion. But then he inexplicably begins to slide away from where I sit with my back pressed against the wall, my chops still held in limp readiness . . . Back. Back. Back he glides until he reaches the entrance where he sidles out into the hall, pulling the door closed after him without a sound.

I jump out of bed and stand for an instant on the cold stone floor. I rush to the door. It's locked! Puzzled I look up to the transom and notice that the lights in the hall are burning as bright as ever. Was he real? Did he exist or have I again confused fantasy with reality? Quietly I slide over the only chair in the room and prop it securely under the door handle—no sense taking any chances—then I grapple again with sleep.

"Huh?" Voices break into my elusive sleep.

"Come on. Get up. We're ready to talk to you," announces the Chairman, rapping his gavel and calling the Group to order.

"Aww," I moan. "Please. Give me a break, willya?" I pull the pillow over my head. "I've got to get some shuteye tonight or I'll go crazy."

"Crazy! Haha," I hear someone titter. Even with my eyes shut I could swear it was Number Two, that erudite phony, laughing in his beard.

"I think you've kept us waiting long enough," says that same voice. And looking up I see, sure enough, old familiar Number Two, his buckteeth glistening through the dark nest of his whiskers like the sharp incisors of a rat.

"Could we at least make this a quicky?" I venture.

"I'm surprised to hear you ask that. You know the rules, Mr. Nudelman," admonishes the Chairman of the Group like a big daddy.

"But I don't! You keep changing them!" I say, throwing down my pillow in frustration.

"Yes!"

"Precisely!"

"*That's* exactly the rules," laughs the Chairman good-naturedly as everyone around the table claps for a brief second.

"Well then, just a short talk," I beg. "Please. If there's any decency in your—"

"T-t-too m-m-much ground t-t-to cover," injects Number Five, the chronic stutterer.

"Well, I'll talk fast."

"All or nothing," warns the Chairman puffing on his pipe. With his bald head and big paunch, double chin and pompous ways, I swear he'd make a perfect double for John Mitchell.

"Perhaps we could reconvene a little later, after Mr. Nudelman has had a chance to rest up a bit," proposes Mrs. J., the middle-aged lady with horn-rimmed glasses and motherly smile.

The Chairman coughs, shuffles his papers in annoyance, then pretends he never even heard the suggestion. Mrs. J., the only lady in the Group, always seems to be causing them trouble. From what I understand, every group has got to have at least one woman in order to satisfy some Federal guideline. I probably would have had a Black in my Group too, except that there just haven't been enough qualified Blacks to go around. So, at least momentarily, the government's relaxed *that* requirement—which does make sense. I suppose they also figured that in my case Negroes just weren't one of my hang-ups. Of course that's a matter of conjecture, "an educated guess," as the Chairman might say. Other than that, however, I don't think my Group is significantly different from anyone else's. If I were forced to describe them I suppose I'd say that, collectively, they are "professional looking." You know, your usual collection of doctors, lawyers, clergy and faggots—the kind of assembly you'd see sitting on a school board, all upright, uptight and terribly boring. And they're always hunched around that formation of curved tables forming a half-moon—just as tonight—passing papers back and forth, sending each other *very important* memos, all in an effort to hide the fact that they're just itching for me to take the stand.

I think the first time I met the Group was in a dream just shortly after being fired from my first job—

"Correction," injects Number Three, a skinny man with bony, vein-lined hands. "It was while you were studying engineering at Brooklyn Polytech."

"Yes. Thank you," says I, trying to sound super polite. As usual, they're right. Brooklyn Poly. That was when I made that first crucial misjudgement, inviting them in. But that night, when they woke me so gently, how was I to know where this would lead? They seemed like such an innocuous, friendly bunch of farts. So, when they said, "Tell us all about yourself," I fell right into the old traperoo. Talked a wild streak. Told them almost everything. They were wonderfully seductive listeners, nodding and yessing, laughing at my jokes and even seemingly touched by the depth of my emotion. Who would have ever guessed that they'd end up using it all against me?

"It's two A.M.," remarks Number Three, nervously scratching one of his marble-white, hairless legs. From where I sit on the edge of my bed I can see them peeking out just above his socks which are held up by green garters. Not many people wear garters these days.

"If you wish, we can excuse you," the Chairman nods in his direction.

"No. No," objects Number Three, a little unconvincingly. "I've been eagerly waiting for this," he says rubbing his hands.

"Oh, fuck off, willya." Annoyed, I roll back into bed, pull the blanket over my shoulders and turn to the wall—as if that would help! These bastards are tenacious, let me tell you.

The Chairman bangs his gavel. "I thought we agreed that we'd have no further infantilism."

"Yeah, that was *last* time," I say smiling. "Remember, my middle name is contradiction. Weren't you the ones who said that?"

"In consideration of Mr. Nudelman's unwillingness to address the Group this evening," recites the Chairman,

114

noisily pulling his chair closer to the table, "and in view of his demonstrated intention to remain uncooperative, I think that we should proceed nonetheless—"

"You can do whatever you want, just leave me out of it. O.K.?" I say, a note of appeal sneaking into my voice despite my resolve not to weaken.

"Unfortunately, you will still be required to listen to the proceedings," grumbles the Chairman.

"We could perhaps come back tomorrow," ventures Number Four a bit meekly.

"Now that's the first intelligent thing I've heard all night," pipes the chief witness, perking up.

"Now. Now. He's becoming defiant," points Number One, putting a check in the appropriate column.

"Stuff it, will you!" I snap. "Just don't start in with that high and mighty crap like you're so much above me. I'll bet you all go home and beat your kids and get dressed up in your wife's undies—or husbands, as the case may be," I bow to Mrs. J. who has a sense of humor. She smiles. Somehow, I've always gotten on better with the women—they're softer, more compassionate, tend to be more open and can even laugh at themselves.

"I move that we adjourn temporarily," says Number One, contemplatively putting his fingers together as is his habit. When you've stood in front of the same Group, year after year, you get to know every little quirk. For instance, Number Six is a chronic nose picker. Number Eight is always furtively adjusting his crotch. Mrs. J., though, has no nervous habits. I really like that woman.

". . .that we leave him to himself until, say five-thirty A.M.," chimes in Number Four, a little too eagerly.

The Chairman nods.

"You'll regret this," sings Number Two, twirling his beard between two fingers as he begins to fade, the others not far behind.

"Hey! Wait! Come back!" I cry. "Look, can't we just have

that *short* discussion? Let's be reasonable. Knowing that you'll be coming back again means I'll be up all night trying to psyche you out, preparing my defense, worrying about just what it is you'll—"

"As you wish," smiles the Chairman, fading back in with a little triumphant smile on his face. "We're very reasonable people. Errr, will the secretary please read the minutes of the last meeting?" he says and Mrs. J. obediently stands up.

"Meeting of the bla bla bla," she begins, mouthing that distorted Report Number Two of their new findings. Bla Bla Bla. I twiddle my thumbs, sit up in bed and play with my toes, cough loudly and blow my nose.

". . . And that Mr. N. will ultimately bring down on himself . . . incorporated in this title . . . but why must he persist in referring to the town he lives in as 'Goobersville' when—as we all know—it has such a lovely name?"

"Thank you. Thank you," smiles the Chairman quite pleased. "Any additions, corrections? Bla Bla? So moved."

Pause.

"Will you please take the stand?" says Mr. Law and Order, dumping the ashes out of his pipe.

"Can I please swear on a Bible this time?" I grin, getting out of bed in my underpants and approaching the bench. The room is so tiny that it takes no more than two steps to reach it.

"If there's one more unnecessary comment or wisecrack," admonishes the Chairman sternly, "we're going to adjourn." At that everybody quickly puts another check in the wisecrack column.

"I'm sorry."

"And feigned contriteness will not be tolerated!" says Number Three, jabbing at me with a bony finger. Boom. There goes another check. Insincerity. What, two checks! Hey, this isn't fair!

"First on the agenda?" asks the Chairman, motioning to Number Five with the end of his gavel.

116

"W-w-we were observing your b-b-behavior with S-S-Stephie," says Number Five.

"I figured as much."

"Sit up straight!" snaps the Chairman. "Stop slouching."

"T-t-tell us how you were l-l-looking at her l-l-legs," utters Number Five, peering deep into my eyes.

"Are you 'gay'?" I grin.

"Answer!"

"I was looking at all of her. At her nose. At her fingernails. At her—"

"At her legs!" shouts Number One.

"Confirmation of body to mind preference," mutters Number Seven.

". . . I was taking her in as a *full* person, an entire human being."

"The legs!" cackles Number Two in his beard.

"You were solely concerned with her body—"

"I object!" I jump up.

"Sit down!" shouts the Chairman.

"Just give me a chance to explain," I begin to sweat, secretly wiping away the perspiration from my upper lip.

"You spent eighty-seven percent of your waking time in her automobile observing her body—we won't even mention the dream part," says Number Six keeping on the pressure.

"You're picking your nose again, Number Six," I try to counterattack.

"Body!" accuses Number One, who looks like a priest.

"No. No," I shake my head. "I was very intrigued by her mind. I've always been fascinated by vegetarians. Anyway, despite what you people think, sex isn't the *only* thing I think about. I do other things. I'm like a camel, I can drink deeply at each oasis. I don't have to stop at every corner just for a sip."

"Come, come," tsks Number Eight.

"O.K. So I looked at her legs. At her body, if you wish. But that's perfectly normal."

"Normal for *you* perhaps," grins Eight, raising his eyebrows victoriously.

"Why, just a moment earlier, did you ask Number Five if he was 'gay'?"

"I meant nothing by it, honestly. I was just trying to be humorous. I wish you'd stop attaching meaning to everything I do or say. And for God's sake stop putting checks in my columns. How will I ever be able to work them off?"

"But that's our job," says Mrs. J., smiling kindly.

"I'd like to further pursue the matter of homosexuality if I may," probes Number One, touching his fingers together again as though in prayer.

"Are you a rabbi?" I ask.

"Why?" asks Number One, digging for meaning.

"What do you mean, 'why'?"

"Would it have any bearing on your position if I were a member of the clergy?"

"No. Just curiosity."

"Supposing I was a rabbi or priest, as you suspect, would it change our relationship? Would you view me more as a father figure than a—"

"Do me a favor and get back on the homo kick. Huh?"

"As you wish . . ." Number One clears his throat and, putting on his glasses, he consults his notes. "We were particularly interested in the way you toyed with the homosexual gentleman who gave you a ride from Binghamton—the one who found it necessary to ask you to step out of his car in Roscoe when you violated the bounds of good taste."

"Oh, him. Look, I've got nothing against fags. I'm super liberal. I just don't want people violating my—"

"The Group will please note the subject's employment of deprecatory and prejudicial appellations."

"But there's no prejudicial intent," I say, pleading against another notation which is (as Perry would say) like pissing

118

against Niagara Falls. "Members of this distinguished group, I appeal to you, I was merely employing the vernacular. I could easily have said fruit or fairy—or, if you'd prefer, even homosexual."

"Yes," nods Number Six, the notorious nose picker, a smile stretching his lips, "But you *didn't*."

"To get back to the homosexual incident under discussion—"

"Homosexual incident?" I cry. "But there was no incident!"

"Your handling of the situation was doubtlessly very cool."

"Doubtlessly," I tiredly shrug—there's just no way to win in a kangaroo court.

"So cool," injects Number Two, "driven to such an extreme that it really represents the flip side of the coin."

"Namely, that by *not* punching out fruits," I say, "for fear of it being a reflection of my own latent homosexuality, I am covering myself by being brazen and super-cool."

"Yes."

"Precisely!"

"Excellent!"

"He *is* learning, isn't he," beams the Chairman. "You know," he nods meaningfully, turning to address the others, "moments like this make me feel as though all our long travails have not been in vain."

"O.K. I confess it. I am a homosexual. I have *always* been. I am the product of a domineering mother and a weak father. My avid interest in heterosexual matters is solely a smokescreen, a clever ruse. Classic syndrome, wouldn't you say? Now, Mr. Chairman, if you'll be so kind as to step into the other room and lower your trousers, I will proceed to bugger you with dispatch."

"Tsk. Tsk," says Number Two, jotting another notation. "Now you're sliding backwards."

"Why do you still find it necessary to attack us?"

119

"Why are you so defensive?"

"So judgemental?"

"Give us a chance. We're your only hope."

"If we don't succeed, you know you'll lose your mind."

"Yes, yes," I sigh sinking down on my bed. I know truth when I hear it. "Look, I'm exhausted. I haven't had a bite to eat since those egg salad sandwiches. My mind is barely functioning. I need to sleep. I gotta meet Mr. Kaufman tomorrow. If I'm not sharp, my goose is cooked, I'm dead. Finished. Last night was torture, too. You people keep coming around more and more often. Please, I'm begging you all for a few nights' peace. Listen, I'll make you a deal. Three days off and I'll go a full marathon. O.K.?"

Silence.

"Look, you've got me so that I'm afraid to go to sleep any more. I mean it. You've got me terrified," I implore with outstretched hands and, though I battle to control myself, I am beginning to weep. Quickly I turn my head from the Group and for a long moment my chest is racked by sobs. I fight to pull myself together, wipe my eyes with my sleeve and then, finally, turn back.

"Do you feel better now?" asks Mrs. J., concerned.

"Not really," I force a tear-stained smile, "but thanks for asking. You're really very kind."

Pause.

"Just what is it you want from me?" I sigh, my reddened eyes going beseechingly from one member of the Group to the next.

"We're coming to that," growls the Chairman.

"Let's go back to the matter of homosexuality," says Number Five picking up the thread, not a shred of mercy in his voice.

"You're on a fishing expedition," I weakly object, "and all at the expense of my time and sleep."

"Have you ever had a homosexual experience," persists Number One.

120

"No. I'm a vegetarian."

"Answer the question!"

"Not really."

"What does *that* mean?"

"Well . . . once—"

"Aha!" chirps Number Four.

"You see! You see!" cries Number Six. "We were right. Mr. Nudelman, you can't fool us."

"If being right is important," I shrug, spent.

"Most certainly," says Mrs. J. "We've got to produce results or we're out of business. You don't think a government agency gets money for nothing, do you?"

"Continue, please," urges the Chairman, watching me with rapt attention.

"Well, when I was thirteen years old I was walking in the woods next to my house in Queens, you know, Forest Park."

"Go on."

"And I met this—"

"D-d-didn't I tell you g-g-gentlemen!" injects Number Five.

"Let him finish!" raps the Chairman.

"And I ran into this guy who managed to corner me in the woods. And he says to me, 'Hey kid, do you want me to do you a favor?' 'What kind of favor?' I ask. 'Do you want me to give you a blow job?' he says."

"Blow job?" questions Number Four, fiddling with his garter.

"Fellatio," explains the Chairman, knowingly.

"Oh," replies Number Four, beginning to scribble furiously.

"And what did you do?" probes Number One, poised and pensive.

"I got scared shit and ran out of the woods as fast as I could."

"He ran!" cried someone.

121

"Ran!" echoed another.

"Ran out of the woods," they are all standing now, chanting and applauding.

"As fast as he could!" screams someone else amid the pandemonium.

I wait uncomfortably for this to end.

"Aha!" exclaims the Chairman finally, after the excitement dies down a bit, and then he begins to scribble something into the record. "Why didn't you tell us that before?"

"Because I didn't attach any significance to it."

"Significance. Let *us* decide that please," he says, gravely concerned.

"But what *does* it mean?"

"I'm sorry but we can't tell you. This goes into the confidential records."

"But I have to know. What about the Freedom of Information Act? I've got a right to know if my character is being maligned. And why is it so vital? Does it mean that I am hetero or homo or what?"

"Its significance certainly goes far beyond such mundane considerations."

"You've got to tell me," I start to cry again, "Please!"

"Now let's get down to the *real* business."

"What business?" I snivel, terror beginning to tighten my throat.

"The ultimate purpose," says Number Seven.

"What are you—?"

"We want a complete confession!" storms the Chairman, violently bringing down his hammer. Desperate, I look at Mrs. J., and suddenly even her eyes have turned cold and fierce.

"Sparing not a sentence nor idea," growls Number One.

"The whole truth and nothing but the truth."

"About what?" I cry.

"You know."

"But I don't! I really don't!"

"Until you confess, there will be no peace."

"I'll confess, but just tell me about what! I honestly don't know."

"But you do."

"About being a queer?"

"No."

"About being unable to love?"

"No."

"About being a worthless shit and social misfit? About being a congenital liar?"

"No."

"No."

"No!"

"But then about what?"

"No hope," says Number Eight, shaking his head in disgust.

"Typical," shrugs Mrs. J., whom I thought was a friend. "You can see it from all the social and psychic indicators."

"Relates to minds not bodies."

"Far too judgemental."

"Can't even hold a job!"

"Couldn't sell bread in a famine."

"But what has this got to do with getting a job?" I cry.

"Nothing and everything!"

"Let us ask the questions!"

"Please," I implore, tears streaming down my face, instinctively attempting to cover my partial nakedness only to discover that I have been standing before this committee in torn underwear—suddenly recalling my mother's warnings always to make sure I had on clean underwear before going for an examination or socks without holes before going to buy shoes.

"Mad as a hatter!" accuses Number Two, pointing at my wretchedness.

"Loonie as a bird!"

"Off his rocker."

"Daffy as a doorknob."

"I'll sign anything. Confess to crimes past and present and imagined. If you'll just give me a—No! I'll confess to nothing. I have my rights! You're just trying to torment me. Give me my dime to call my lawyer. Anyhow, none of this counts because you forgot to read me my rights," I shout at them, waving my fist in the air. "I'm no dummy. I know the law."

"Nuttier than a fruitcake."

"I move that this case be dismissed on grounds that—!"

"Whackier than a woodpecker!"

"O.K. I'll confess. But damn it, if I start there'll be no end. We'll be here till doomsday."

"We've got plenty of time," smiles the Chairman.

"But what in the world is it that I have to confess?"

"You'll see, Mr. Nudelman," he laughs as they begin to fade out. "You'll see."

With the Group gone, I am left stranded and confused in the middle of my windowless nook in the Y, still clad in ragged underwear—certainly no way to testify before a distinguished panel, but they do have a way of popping up at the most inopportune moments. Had I stayed at a decent hotel—even put up at my mother's flat with its pink carpets, plastic flowers and lush, nouveau-bordello furnishings— chances are good that they'd have spared me tonight. Let that be a lesson . . . I pace the room, trundle out into the hall and then head for the men's room (as if there were a ladies' room here. Haha. Very funny, Mr. Nudelman. One minute you're bawling, the next you're cracking jokes).

Save for the sound of tinkling water, the bathroom is deserted—long lines of sinks and urinals stand in dribbling readiness like anxious sentinels. Three-thirty A.M. Even voyeurs have to get a little shuteye—probably busy creating new fantasies based on yesterday's prick observations.

Standing in obeisance before one of the porcelain urns I take a pee in a long, gorgeous golden arch that would put even McDonald's to shame. I pull the lever and watch with drugged fascination as the cascading and swirling water does its work. Fine American plumbing, I shake my head in admiration. Still though, I've got to get out of this joint. If I try to sleep here again there's no telling. The Group's liable to break all precedent and come back for a second round in the same night. It's this fleabag flophouse that's getting to me. No doubt about it. I shake my head, bone weary. Why am I always a boarder on the seamy edge of life, a perennial resident of the wrong side of the tracks? What I most need now—at this sad juncture in my personal, familial and financial history—is a little fun in my life. Fun. F.U.N. Whatever that's supposed to be. Though I'm afraid if I ran smack into it, if it grabbed me by the nuts and tickled my armpits, I still wouldn't be able to recognize it. Fun, that is. But everyone's always talking about it, right? Come on over to my house and we'll have some *fun*. Boy, wasn't last night *fun*? Haven't had so much *fun* in years. For the life of me I still can't figure out what it is, though I know that everyone ought to have a little of it, and I certainly can't think of anyone more deserving than yours truly. FUN. It's as elusive as success. Now there's another one, I think, chugging back into my cubbyhole, my addled brain uncovering fresh profundities at a truly startling rate. If only I had a pen, piece of paper, a small amount of patience and a disgusting amount of conviction, it'd make fascinating reading. Why bother with novels? Assembled under the guise of a collection of intellectual essays or a philosophical tract, it'd probably bring me not only a Nobel prize, but also some *fun* and maybe even—if I'm real good and behave myself—a little *success*. Naah. What I need to do is write a best seller, write a fast-paced novel about a guppy that terrifies a small, isolated community.

I dress, pack my bag and head downstairs—already feeling distinctly better as I leave the room for good. In the lobby I make a beeline to a phone booth and call Goobersville. The phone rings. Rings. Rings.

"Hello?" comes Viveca's voice, deep and bathed in sleep.

"It's me," I chirp, magically rejuvenated by the mere sound of her voice.

"What's the matter?" she asks, a little dazed.

"Nothing. I'm fine."

"But—"

"Everything's fine. Really. I'm even having FUN. I just had to tell you one thing and ask another."

"Huh?" she yawns.

"I just called to tell you that I love you madly, insanely, even devotedly."

"At—At four o'clock in the morning?" she laughs, her laughter a sweet contrast to my abysmal surroundings.

"Don't ask me to explain."

"I'm touched."

"Bullshit."

"Really. It's just that I'm still half asleep. You woke me in the middle of an exciting dream."

"What kind of dream? Erotic? Was I in it?"

"Yes and no."

"Tell me about it."

"No!"

"Why must you be so cryptic? Tease but never tell, that's you. But this is business!"

"No."

"I've always thought that if you could somehow record a woman's dreams, especially her sex dreams, it'd make a powerful book—not to mention a fortune."

"And what was the 'other thing' you called about?" she asks, failing to nibble at the bait.

"Yes. The other matter. Please inquire of Magnus if he has a message for me?"

"But he's fast—"

"Asleep. I know. That's exactly the point. You won't be bothering him. Just ask him if he has tonight's message for Daddy," I explain and wait while Viveca reluctantly goes to the kiddy room.

When she comes back to the phone she is chuckling. "With his eyes shut and a smile on his face," she laughs, "he says, 'Children are slaves.' "

"Excellent. Thanks. See you," I say, hanging up and pulling a disappearing act before the operator can hit me for the overtime.

Yes. To the point. Children are slaves. Last night, Magnus

gave me the sleep message that "We are barbarians." How does a six-year-old pick up lingo like that? And what does he mean? Was he referring to children, or us as a family, or the whole human race? Such profundities, I think as I stroll down Second Avenue in the brisk night air, the streets empty except for an occasional taxi. The night has turned crystalline, so clear, in fact, that despite the city lights I can make out stars winking to me from between the high rooftops.

I check my watch. Four-fifteen . . . Hmmm . . . If I am, by chance, to arrive at Bernie's office just before lunch, that gives me a good eight hours . . . Think of it, eight whole hours to do with as I see fit, to indulge my every whim. Let's see . . . I could of course go to the zoo, but I think all its inhabitants except for the bats are sleeping. Then there's the bus terminal, subways, train stations and all-night eateries—though the latter could prove a wee bit difficult without taking a bite. What with Bernie inviting me to an extravagant lunch—though he still doesn't know it— I'd hate to spoil my appetite. Too, it's best to save a few nickles. 'Waste not, want not,' I reason, thumbing through my wallet and checking every pocket for loose coins. Let's see . . . Started off with all the family reserves minus the usual five emergency dollars left with Viveca (in case one of the kids comes down with some horrible disease requiring some immediate life-giving medicine). That means I walked out the door with twenty-six dollars and forty-three cents. Spent three-fifty at the Y (I knew I was going to regret that hasty move. Damn it! If I had skipped the Y I could have splurged on a lavish breakfast—though chances are that with that money safe in my pocket I wouldn't have spent it, cheap sonofabitch that I have become.) Eighty-five cents for the call . . . That should leave twenty-two dollars . . . and . . . eight cents, I calculate in my head as I continue to march downtown, so wrapped up in finances that I am oblivious to my surroundings.

128

Twenty-two dollars and eight cents. What used to be cigar money has mushroomed into a week's groceries. But why despair? At worst this is all temporary. Even John Paul Getty was probably reduced to counting nickels—maybe even pennies—when he was first starting out. Twenty-two dollars and eight cents—essentially our net worth if you don't count all the outstanding bills, debts and mortgage. Let's call it twenty-three for argument's sake. Do you know, Nudelman, that there are people living this very day who could fork over that or more to a doorman without batting an eyelash. Or slip a twenty to a poor schwarze who's holding out a stick of soap and a towel in some fancy nightclub pissoir. Or use it to light a cigar or wipe their ass. And here you are counting pennies. Doesn't it make you feel like the abominable turd that you are? Not at all. This is all a transitory discomfort. Later, when I am infinitely wealthy, I will write nostalgically about these dog days. Together Viveca and I will recall "those hard times" much as Pat and Richard Nixon were always recounting those early years when he was still patching flats in Daddy's gas station and Pat was forced to work nights as a bartender. And though the Nixons have expressed nothing but bitterness for those leaner years, I will look back with a distant and sentimental smile, fondly recalling those "meaningful" times when life was simpler, when I had but trifles to worry about, when I didn't have to trouble myself scouring the day's market for tax exempt government bonds, building tax shelters or tearing down existing fiscal laws.

Twenty-two dollars and eight cents. Tell me, Bernie, if you checked into the Y and dropped three-fifty, would you still be whining about it eight hours later?

"Three-fifty?" laughs Bernie. "You mean three hundred and fifty thousand, don't you?"

"Yes. Yes," I laugh. "Of course. I always misplace those damn floating decimal points. I used to be a mathematician, Bernie, can you believe it? Well, we're just off by a factor of ten to the fifth power. And what's a few zeroes among friends," I chide, breaking into wild laughter as I dig into my pocket and come up with only twenty-one dollars and eighty-five cents. "We're missing twenty-three, Bernie. Twenty-three thousand, of course. Where did they disappear to? Foul play?" I mutter aloud, passing a cop who has been closely observing me for a block. What's the matter. Hasn't he ever seen someone talking to himself? Poor schmuck must be on the streets fresh out of police school. Give him another two weeks and he'll be holding brilliant conversations with his night stick.

Twenty-one eighty-five. Seven hours to blow. Bernie, you've got to come through with some money today or I'm fucked. Seven hours . . . No, six-and-a-half . . . Time flies . . . Then six . . . In my sleep-deprived stupor I'm still not sure where I'm going, but before I can begin to figure out the day's program, I realize that my feet have already transported me all the way down to lower Manhattan and I'm weeding through the tangle of feet of winos dozing in shop doorways. The Bowery. It was here that my father took me and my big brother, Walter, for a little reality therapy. "Take a good look," said Daddy, motioning to some snoozing drunks. "This is where you'll end up if you don't do your homework. In the gutter!" It scared the living shit out of Walter, terrified him straight into the tentacles of graduate school and a Ph.D. I, on the other hand, was somehow impressed that these snoring individuals were not plagued by my father's problems. They had no rent, no overhead to speak of, usually got a decent night's sleep, and—destitute as they were—had neither to slave twelve-hour days nor live in imminent terror, trying to predict just exactly when the crumbling artifice of their printing company would come crashing down around their ears. Damn it! Why was I always such a smart-ass? Why couldn't I have been frightened and bamboozled like Walt all the way into my Ph.D.? A little more terror and maybe I would have

131

made it? Perhaps even gone on for a little postdoctoral work. Today I'd be secure, rich and miserable like all my other scientific friends. Instead I'm insecure, poverty-stricken and happy. Being poor is romantic, right? Ah yes, the times when Viveca and I were penniless were the best days of our lives. We lived from hand to mouth, but we loved each other. Like a team of oxen we pulled our load together. Never a harsh word. Never a tear. Stoical, brave, thrifty, kind, that was us. Friendly, courteous, considerate, obedient—everything a boy scout or a dog should be.

'A little more, a few more blocks,' prod my feet, taking me along the eastern edge of Chinatown, the air still pungent with last night's Moo Goo Gai Pan. A little further downtown and, lo and behold, suddenly I look up to discover a vast artwork of spun steel cables draped over long stone towers.

The Brooklyn Bridge! I mumble and gazing up at those familiar graceful arcs swooping off into the darkness I am swamped by a cascade of forgotten memories. The Brooklyn Bridge, utter I in the premorning darkness as a lone car darts along the curving roadway, its red taillights flying across the span to the other shore where Brooklyn waits, glistening seductively in speckled lights like a painted whore.

Kings County. It was here as a promising thirteen-year-old blackmarketeer that I used to make my pick-up, trading in illegal fireworks as others deal in hot diamonds or heavy dope. I was crafty in those days, let me tell you. With such a glorious beginning I should have gone on to Saigon or Beirut or, at the very least, become a graft-prone elevator inspector.

Yes. Brooklyn Bridge. The sleepy mind keeps straying. It was here that I often fled between classes at Brooklyn Polytech where they were busily grooming me for an electronic oblivion; here, to this bridge, that I hurried to clear a head spinning with Differential Calculus and Quantum Mechanics and Field Theory Equations; here that

132

I used to come to stroll the walkways, munching on a dry sandwich my mother had so dutifully thrown together, here on this span that I would gaze down at the tugs pulling scows of garbage through the oil slicks and floating debris. Fall. Winter. Spring. Somehow, hanging over the bridge was better than hanging around Poly's lawn of green-painted concrete. Sure, the East River was a cesspool. But to me it smelt sea-like fragrant compared to that building, sour with the sweat of a thousand tooling engineers, that technical edifice that in happier times had been a Gillette razor blade factory. Razor blades! Third time tonight, I note, climbing up the long arch of the first suspension cable, balancing on the icy line with my overnight bag in one hand. I used to be quite a mountain goat as a kid.

Easing my way up in the near darkness, alternate patches of light and shadow cast across my path, I ascend the steepening cable. Up. Up. I pause. Take a deep breath. The air tastes of seaweed and brine, exotic ships and foreign cargoes. Up. Up. Still up. This is where I belong; I should have checked in here instead of the Y and saved those precious three-and-a-half smackeroos.

Removing my belt and hitching my bag around the back of my waist, I now take off on the sheer part of the climb where the last section of cable rises near vertically. Brooklyn Bridge, I chant as though hypnotized, while a hundred or so feet below me a car bounces along the roadway. And far, far below there's actually a tug out tonight, tiny as a toy with little lights on its bow and stern, chugging up the ice-choked river. A cold wind rushes down the water and, whistling through the wires of the bridge, blows my hair on end like the wildman hottentot I have become. "Oolagoolanimbarumba," I whisper to the bridge, informing her that a friend is on the way up.

Up. Up. Like a lithe cat I slink up the cold steel line. I am a jungle cheetah, a lynx, the last of the great monkeymen. Ha! Let the Group come up here if they want a meeting. Let

133

them find a place to set up those stately, curved, oak tables of theirs, if they can.

Up. Up. Up. Skyward I shinny like Spiderman, Batman, Wonderwoman rolled into one; like Captain Marvel, Superman, The Lone Ranger and Malcolm X. Look Mama, it's me, your son, Red Ryder, Roy Rogers, Gene Autry and Ronald Reagan, all in one agile and fearless human frame. Aren't you proud of me now? Dad, I never told you this because I was sworn to secrecy, but the *real* reason I never finished my Ph.D. is that—unbeknownst to you—I am, in *real* life, none other than the Green Hornet. Feigning the appearance of a mild-mannered bum, I have actually been extraordinarily busy saving lives, rescuing maidens in distress and rewriting illiterate pornographic novels.

Then suddenly, before you can whisper Shazaam, I am reaching out, touching the stone parapets of the suspension tower and discovering—as though it had been made specifically for me—a little nook carved out of the tower wall, a nest hollowed into the face of the fortress with barely enough space for a lean monkeyman.

I climb in and, sheltered from the fierce wind, I now feel wonderfully warm sitting balanced between two boroughs; no-man's land, the end of the world. From my vantage, invisible to the rest of the world, I can look all the way up the east shore of the city, make out the lights on the Manhattan, Williamsburg and even the Queensborough bridges. The other way I can see Staten Island and the Verrazano Narrows, while to the northwest I could swear, with the morning still so dark yet transparent, I can make out the steep palisades of New Jersey. New Joisey.

I lean back, light up a last cigarette and glance down past my feet to discover a nearby rooftop sign blazingly proclaiming "Jehovah's Kingdom." Heaven on earth, I think, taking a long contented drag. I watch the cigarette end glow in the dark and then, seized by impulse, I toss it far out into the night and follow it with trance-like fascination as it tumbles, the wind playfully sweeping it up as it tries to fall . . . Dear God in Heaven, I pray, turning momentarily religious, please let Bernie, my Savior, bail me out. If you help me this *one* time, I'll never again beat my kids, I will stay sober, cease all philandering, and will even love, honor and treasure my neighbors. Thank you. Amen.

"If, as you believe, God is really controlling your life," said Viveca last week, "then you, or we, must have done something very wrong."

"God is superstitious," says Leif, meaning that He is the figment of human fears.

"A lot of dead people live around here," observes Magnus sagaciously as we drive to Goobersville, passing a long mile of cemetery.

. . . For a few minutes I take a quick snooze and then, opening my eyes, I am pleased to discover the faintest hint of blue. Morning. A band of reddish-yellow begins to burn above Brooklyn. I've just about made it, I crow, feeling the first tentative pulses of life, hearing alarm clocks going off across the city like fusillades of cannon, sensing the stretches and yawns of a million-and-one fuzzy-mouthed souls as they turn in their boxes like snug little hamsters, sleepily scratching their armpits and bellies and dandruffy hair.

Another day.

.   .   .

Seven-thirty and they're off and running, traffic on the bridge bumper to bumper. From our roving helicopter we can see all the major parkways, streets and alleys at a standstill. As a result of spiraling cabbage prices there is a serious gas shortage. Electricity is a no-no since all the municipal electrons have gone on a wildcat strike. The Mayor, having recently gone gaga, is storming around his

135

mansion in just socks and tennis shoes, pulling out what's left of his hair. With apoplectic, bulging eyes, the Governor has just gone on television to declare a state of emergency, a state of unrest and a state of the union. As far as the weather's concerned, things don't look much better. The forecast is promising low visibility, low employment and low punches. During the afternoon there will be falling temperatures, falling barometers and falling arches. There'll be ill winds blowing in from the east and plenty of hot air from the south. For tomorrow the weatherman is calling for much of the same, a stationary low pressure system having settled in over the world to give us, for the indefinite future, continued low salaries and high levels of misery.

Ah, New York, city of shattered dreams and pox. On a morning like this, the red sky in the east merging with a line of beige Jersey smog, one could almost want to live here. Yes. Right here. This is where I belong, on this bridge, directing traffic and raising a little bedlam. Why, for twelve years, have I hidden myself away like a monk in the Goobersville woods? *Action*, as Leif craves, that's what I need. How is it that a man who has sailed the seven seas, gazed on the bare breasts of dark maidens, crossed continents by camel, roamed Asia and rediscovered Africa, how is it possible that he has succumbed to burying himself in lovely Goobersville? Goobersville. Yeech! You want to know why? Because he's nuttier than a fruitcake. The Group was right for once—gotta hand it to them, nuttier than a— Oh God! What an idea! I slap my forehead. Thick-headed, unworthy and ungrateful creep that I am, the Group was trying to do me a favor, hand me a brainstorm on a platter. Daffier than a doorknob, they said. Loonier than a—. But of course! For once that assemblage of chronic nose-pickers and beard-twiddlers has provided me with inspiration: cultivate your insanities, they were saying. Go whole hog. Declare your madness. If necessary take out a full page ad in the *Times*. Foam at the mouth and snap at ankles. Stick out your tongue like a homunculus and roll your eyes like marbles. Wonderful! Genius!

"I've got to get to a phone, fast," I mumble, gathering up my goods and climbing back out on the cable—the icy wind coming up to greet me. . .

Down. Down. Down, I cautiously slide backwards, cars stopping and jamming up as I near the roadway and take one last leap, landing on feet that crumble from the impact. Picking up myself and my bag I race down the bridge until I come to it: a telephone. For emergencies only. If survival does not qualify as an emergency, then what does?

411. Information. I get that special number with the speed of summer lightning, my heart still pounding away, my mind reeling from the profundity of my simple realization. I dial, my frozen but greedy fingers hard at work. A dime invested, a fortune earned.

"Hello? Social Security? I am calling for the family of a friend who has just had a nervous breakdown. No-no. The friend. Right. Nice guy, but nuttier than a fruitcake—if you know what I mean. Haha. Could you please tell me what the criteria are for receiving disability benefits?"

.   .   .

Such criteria, I laugh, hugging myself with joy as I waltz down the streets of lower Manhattan. My friend—the one with the disintegration of all systems—will flunk the sanity test with flying colors. Simply stated—for the benefit of that same friend who has trouble seeing the obvious—in order to qualify for disability payments he must have a medically established condition which makes it impossible for him to work for a year or more. Haha. And if I know him right he will opt for 'the more'. Now, since our friend meets the "insured status requirement," having worked twenty quarters out of the last forty, all that remains is for him to surrender himself at the Goobersville Mental Hygiene Clinic. A mere formality. A trifle. One look at him—he needn't even list the symptoms—and they'll be down on their knees begging him to accept those disability checks. What was it Freud said about the proximity of neurosis and the creative arts? Anyway, I'm a great actor. And for once in my life I've got everything going for me.

Social Security, I shake my head in wonderment. And it's not like Welfare. For eons I have poured money into those golden coffers. Now I will simply be borrowing a little of *my* money till things improve. Eons? O.K., ten years. But why quibble over little matters like time when we still have a full three hours until we dine with Uncle Bernie? And anyway, why get so moralistic? Other countries have generous programs to help struggling artists. The only difference here will be that this government will be 'supporting the arts' without being aware of its noble philanthropy.

With morning now fully arrived, splashing forth in color and song, I suddenly realize that now—at this very instant in time—I stand at the turning point of my existence with all fiscal indicators pointing upward, my personal condition strongly bullish. In but a matter of minutes, I have undergone a spontaneous and profound resurrection. Never again will I be forced to undergo the humiliation of having to count pennies. Nor, for that matter, will I have to stay in sleazy inns, experience foodless meals, be at the mercy of whimsical elements or wait for a benevolent handout. Goodbye Spaghetti-O's, hello pâté. There will be new ten-speed bikes for each of the boys. Viveca will have to be thoroughly retrained in the art of consuming. For my part, I will simply lean back—somewhere on that sun-drenched beach near Nice or Cannes—and watch as my children romp in the waves. I will become the picture of brown contentment, endlessly shoveling salad Nicoise into my fat face. I will have all my teeth filled, my underpants sewn, my heart and cancer conditions permanently cured. I will drink nothing but the finest of booze, sip aperitifs like a king, dress in only hand-tailored suits of linen. Now, with everything golden, all I need to do is get Bernie to put up a little front money to keep me going until those checks start rolling in, a few Scheckels to tide me over before the deluge of payments. Whhheeew! I whistle, click my heels in the air, feel on top of the world. For once I will return to Goobersville with new-found vigor. Who knows, with my good fortune strong as it is, maybe the Szorskys will open a can of peas filled with botulism. Have themselves a nice Sunday dinner. In this world of infinite and wonderful possibilities, surely *anything* can happen.

It is with high hopes and faint heart (now there's another prize-winning Kaufman title) that I enter the offices of BERNARD J. KAUFMAN & ASSOCIATES. Pretty fancy digs. I admire the lush, plush, lavish outer office, the room festooned with posters of cavity-free teeth, people holding their heads in various stages of Excedrin headaches, and dogs smiling over cans of all-meat dog food. Fancy-Schmancy, I whistle, seeing Bernie's name in two-foot letters jutting out against a wall of baby-blue, the floor deep in white carpets that must have consumed the skins of eight hundred poodles.

BERNARD J. KAUFMAN & ASSOCIATES. What a layout! Sure, I figured he had a comfortable office, but nothing like *this*. By comparison, this outer office alone would make a Pharaoh's chambers look like the public pissoir in the B.M.T. I'm truly impressed. Eyeing the deep leather sofas it's apparent that I should have slept here last night. Such utter luxury, I think, dusting the seat of my trousers before slowly sitting down, sinking down into this wealth of foam, losing myself in cushions of rich, brown leather. Hmmm. Just smell them. If I had an outer office like this I'd never go into the inner one, much less work, I reason, jumping up and down to make sure this is all real— one can never be too careful these days.

"Sir, may I help you?" inquires a polite receptionist who, I could swear, looks like one of the hookers I used to watch on 59th Street before some outraged citizens had the cops put on the muscle.

"Yes . . . Well," I mumble confused, standing up and glancing at the man with the Excedrin headache. "Has Mr. Kaufman gone to lunch yet?" I ask, while my brain begins feverishly figuring how I'm going to handle this interview . . . Should I make a complete confession and disclosure, fall on my knees in front of Mr. Kaufman's desk, contritely prostrating myself on his poodle-white carpets as I beg for a second chance? Or do I play it cool, Madison Avenue style, explaining that the new "Hearts and Hymens" package is a concept that must be examined in entirety, market-tested on individuals from all strata, classes, and creeds within this great society before simply rejecting its basic premise? Do I cajole Bernie? Do I pamper his whims? Do I play the hard-boiled novelist with jaded eyes and jaundiced liver who's seen it all, unphased by baby-blue walls and real honest-to-goodness leather sofas.

"Sir?" says Bernie's hooker, waking me from my reverie. "Shall I—"

"Just tell him that Pete Miller is here. Haha."

"And—"

"No. No! I was just joking. It's an in-joke. On second thought tell him that—" Shall I give him my real name? Maybe he's so disgusted that I won't even get through that massive oak door. Be brave, what do you have to lose? What? Eight hundred dollars. A king's ransom. Oh, God, why did I fuck around with his novel? It was cruel, vicious, inconsiderate and uneconomical. Who am I to play with other people's fondest—

"Who then shall I say—?"

"Say. . .Say that Mr. Nudelman is here to see him," I sigh, sinking back down into those deep cushions, hoping to be swallowed alive.

". . .A Mr. Nudelman here to—"

"Nudelman? Yeah. Just the man I want to see. Send him right in." I hear Mr. Bernard Kaufman & Associates' voice echo through the transistorized box.

"You can—"

"Yes," I nod, feigning a smile as I quickly straighten my clothes and stash my suitcase with its broken zipper behind one of the sofas. The girl has been watching my little performance. Quickly, I check myself in the mirror. How do I look? Do I look seedy or do I look artistic? Do I appear like I've come to get something or give something?

"Come in, come in," crows Captain Bernie as I gently knock on the door marked "President". President! I am Erlichman, Haldeman, John Dean and Chuck Colson come to pay homage to my Commander-in-Chief, my hat in my hand, prepared to do his bidding, do whatever is expedient, anything to keep from enraging my superior. Only now can I begin to understand what those poor, tortured men must have gone through. Anything for a few Scheckels, a job, a position, a modest estate in Georgetown.

"Good to see you," calls the voice of President Kaufman, who holds over yours truly the power of life and death, in addition to the strings to eight hundred crisp dollars of mine.

And then I am standing in *His* office, searching the long room for Bernie Kaufman, knowing that somewhere amidst the miles of shelves and aisles cluttered with products and geegaws, sits President Kaufman. "Come in," he calls again, finally making himself visible by rising up from behind a desk that is inundated with cans and bottles and tubes and cartons. And though standing, Bernie—who had impressed me as such a tall, stately man—is dwarfed in an office that looks like a drug store crammed with bargains. Lying in piles and heaps, propped up in neat lines or balanced on the edges of the ubiquitous shelves, are products sufficient to satisfy the needs of a vast army suffering from irregularity, athlete's foot, hemorrhoids and iron poor blood.

"Sit down. Don't be bashful," beams B. Kaufman, proprietor of this great supermarket of bandaids, beach balls and bubble bath—shopkeeping perhaps a spicy little sideline

142

to keep him happy when accumulating companies gets dull.

"What's all this? I finally ask.

"Clients," explains Bernie reverently with outstretched hands.

"Oh. I see," I nod, wandering up and down the rows of this fortieth floor boutique, sampling a squirt of Old Spice, a little spray of Self-Styling Adorn, a quick whiff of a premixed douche as I try to forestall my execution.

"Now," says Bernie a little later, allowing time for me to satisfy my curiosity. "About *Hearts and Hymens*—"

"And what's this?" I stall, picking up a bottle. "Compound W. Hmmm . . . 'helps dissolve warts away' . . . What a pity I don't have any—"

"About *Hearts and*—"

"Look, I want to explain about that," I suddenly turn to face my accuser, my heart in my mouth, though I feel mildly intoxicated from all the aerosols.

"What's there to explain?" questions Mr. K., jutting out his lower lip.

"I just wanted to tell you why I changed it, and—"

"Listen, I don't care *why* you changed it or *how* you changed it or *what* went through your head. The only thing I want is for you to keep doing exactly what you've been doing." '

"Huh? But I thought that—"

"And I thought so, too!" says Bernie, shrugging his shoulders and laughing. "But the publishers loved it."

"What?" I ask, flabbergasted, beginning to wonder if this is just another ruse engineered by the Group.

"Listen, in business you've got to be big enough to admit it when you're wrong. It's the key to success. And I was wrong!"

"What happened?"

"It's really very simple. After I told Mr. Z. about being dismayed with your rewrite, he insisted I send it over to his office anyhow. He then sent it to an editor who read it in one sitting—she couldn't stop—and then passed it on to two others in the same house. That same afternoon they were back on the phone to Mr. Z., unanimous in their appraisal."

"Unanimous?"

"Raving!"

"Raving?"

"The funniest thing they'd ever read. They called it 'Porn with humor'—though I certainly don't appreciate the label."

"Certainly not," says I, shaking my head in earnest disgust while fighting to keep a straight face.

"But look, if it sells . . ." smiles Bernie.

"If it smells . . ." echoes yours truly.

"Then it's got to be good."

"Just gotta be."

"I'm terribly pleased," says Bernie, lurching across the desk to grab my hand.

"Look, don't thank me," I answer a little sheepishly as he holds on, "It's your book."

"No."

"No?"

"It's *our* book. I've decided that we'll have both our names on the cover."

"Well. . .That's certainly very generous of you," I hedge, determined never to be publicly connected with either a heart, hymen, or combination thereof. "Would that mean that I get a share of the advance?" I probe.

"Naturally, I expect that we'll stick to our original contract," says Mr. K. meaning, of course, no.

"Oh," says I, a little disheartened . . . "No, I just couldn't do it," I shake my head, "couldn't infringe on your rights as *the* author. I'm only making minor changes," says I, extending my hands heavenward in a gesture of magnanimity.

"Well, I can't tell you how happy I am," beams Bernie. "Here. Wait! Before you leave, let me give you some items to take home," says the President, jumping up. "Come, follow me," he cries, marching down the aisles as I obediently follow him, arms outstretched. "Take some Tanfastic for the next time you go to Puerto Rico," he says, plucking a handful off the shelf. "Here, have some Gleem. And some of this. Some of these. A little of this . . . And this . . . And this . . ." he says, as we drunkenly weave up and down the aisles, Bernie grabbing at random, demonstrating his gratitude in a shower of bottles of Anacin and Grease Relief, boxes of Stay-free Minipads and Digel, not to mention containers of Mop & Glo as well as a carton of Friskies Buffet—all seventeen meals. "And take one of these. And these. And . . . these!" sings Bernie Kaufman, master of ceremonies, loading me up like a donkey on a give-away show, my arms bulging with gifts. And with bottles and aerosol cans and plastic dispensers tumbling off the precarious pile onto the poodle rugs, I bend down to greedily scoop up the valuable merchandise as Uncle Bernie continues to load on his appreciation non-stop. "Here, have some Listerine—tastes awful, but sure is effective," he jokes, mimicking the commercial. "And here some—No, you don't need this," he says, tossing back the Dentugrip.

"No. No. Pile it on," I venture, fearful of missing out on something *free*. "And how about some Adolph's Meat Tenderizer," I suggest. Or a couple of rolls of Bounty, "the quicker picker-upper?" And what about a little Raid that "kills bugs dead?" Yes. Yes. More. More. Spare me nothing. A little Maybelline Ultra Lash, a little Earthborn Natural pH. Amen and praise the Lord. Time is running out. Got to get saved. If I can get enough of this stuff together maybe I can open up a pharmacy in Goobersville. Sure I can use it Bernie, just throw it on. And who doesn't need a higher level of pain relief? And what man in his right mind doesn't want his underpants smelling April fresh or to have protein washed into his hair. And if I can't use the body-giving protein I can always pass it on to some poor kwashiorkor victim in Bangladesh.

"Enough?" laughs Bernie, surveying me as I lie exhausted in a pile of produce that would give any self-respecting housewife multiple orgasms.

"Yes! Enough. Enough," I laugh. What more could any decent human being ask for (besides lunch and a little badly needed predisability money)? Just think of it . . . Thanks to the combined efforts of American industry, B. Kaufman & Associates and Wisk, I will never again suffer the embarrassment of ring-around-the-collar. Also, with great gratitude to a couple of those same benefactors, I will now start taking a regular regimen of life-giving Geritol tablets and liquid which, incidentally, have more than twice the iron of any ordinary supplement. I will use Visine with tetrahydrozoline to get the red out. I will fight drops that spot with Cascade. My skin will glow with Avon's Moisture Secret. I will relish every juicy morsel of Alpo Dog Food, which is all meat and contains not a drop of soy protein or grain filler—just read the label. Each morning I will simultaneously gargle with Lavoris, Scope and Cepacol while inundating my armpits with Arrid Extra Dry, Secret and Sure. I will sport No-Nonsense Pantyhose, sterilize my toilet bowl with Vanish and employ Magic Prewash to remove my grease, grass and ravioli stains.

And finally, to top things off when life in Goobersville becomes a bit dull, I will open my box of Betty Crocker's Ready-to-spread Frosting, open it and spread!

"Isn't it time for lunch?" I suggest, casually checking my non-existent watch, the image of luscious, imitation chocolate fudge triggering the eternal juices of my mouth.

.   .   .

Lunch is a simple affair, your usual businessman's mid-day snack of wine and juicy red steak, heart of artichokes and hot bread whisked fresh out of the oven. There is a

146

dessert of multiple layer cake or exotic flavored ice cream or an exquisite pudding—all of which I must sample. The President and I are sitting at one of the intimate tables that line the walls, surrounded on both flanks by well-dressed exec types casually nibbling their mid-day repast—a perfect setting, to say the very least, for discussing business.

"I've been doing a little thinking," says Mr. N., wiping the remains of pudding from the corners of his mouth and sucking clean a few offending fingertips. "Actually, I've been wondering," stalls this master of procrastination, ". . . about the money for the rewrite."

"Oh?" inquires Bernie, dabbing his lips and lifting a wary eyebrow.

"I was thinking," says I, somehow losing courage, "that, what with the rewrite receiving such favorable readings, that . . . perhaps, you could . . ."

"Give you an advance?" ventures Mr. K.

"Precisely. You took the words out of my mouth," I smile, forcing an amiable, though nervous little laugh.

Bernie chuckles.

"We could pro-rate the amount," I suggest a bit meekly.

"Yes, we could," says Mr. Kaufman. "But I've always believed in sticking to a contract—to the letter. Don't you?"

"Of course," I answer, a little too quickly, a little too defensively.

"My feeling is that if you start making changes on one—"

"You'll start doing it on all," I chime in. "I agree."

"Business is business."

"Absolutely. Certainly. Except this is art."

For a moment there is a pregnant silence, Bernie and I sizing each other up, as the waiter slips the check onto the table.

"Do you need money?" asks Bernie, looking me deep in the eye, and for a second I see more than just Bernard Kaufman, peddler of cosmetics and acquirer of companies. For that brief instant I somehow detect little cracks in that

147

impeccably smooth facade—little fissures revealing specks of humaneness, a vulnerability I have never seen before in this man I have painted in my own mind as no more than a commercial clown. Peering back into his eyes—if I am not deceiving myself—I see weakness and tragedy, and he is asking me if my life, too, borders on the tragic. Do I need money, he is asking? Am I poor? Am I down and out? On the skids? Do I wear the clothes that I do because I am a madman Bohemian, or is it because I can't afford fancier rags? Do I gobble victuals like an Auschwitz victim because I am desperately hungry, or am I just a sinewy glutton? Somehow this most ordinary of questions cuts me to the quick. Do I need money? It is a question that is both kind and yet reeks of complicity. Of course I need money, I try to shout, but I have turned into a mute. If I had money I could look into Bernie's eyes and say *yes*, sure, I need money. But I have none and, therefore, I can't! Does it make sense? Of course not. Nothing makes sense any more. I am so twisted and insanely defensive that issuing a simple declarative sentence, making an admission that's as clear as the nose on my face is an impossibility. "Do you?" repeats Bernie.

"Doesn't everybody," laughs Mr. N., reaching for the check.

"No," objects Bernie, making a quick grab for the paper, "Let me—"

"No. No," argues Mr. N., hanging onto the tab for dear life. "You paid last time, this time it's—" he gasps, seeing a bill for eighteen dollars and thirty cents dancing in front of his bloodshot eyes.

"I insist," argues Bernie, trying again for the check.

"Absolutely not!" persists Mr. N., already digging into his wallet and quickly counting out eighteen for the courteous waiter who casually accepts the payment as if it consisted of just your everyday collection of dollar notes. And here's a generous gratuity for you, sir, for such excellent service, scurrying as you did back and forth to the kitchen to satisfy our every whim; here's another three crisp ones for all those invaluable errands we harried businessmen could not perform for ourselves, for all those refills of ice water, for that second cup of coffee, for the forks and knives and napkins—all those little extras that spell fine service.

"Thanks for lunch," nods Bernie appreciatively, getting up and buttoning his jacket around his belly.

Mr. N., big spender with fifty-three cents left in his trousers waves away gratitude. It was nothing. Who needs money? You know what money is? It's crap, that's what it is! It soils the possessor. Yeech. Anyway, it was my turn to treat. Fair is fair. Can't always be a pig on the take, can we? Sometimes a man has got to be a man and stand drinks, too, right? Right!

Bernie and I step out onto the sidewalk. Together we look up at the sky which has turned as abysmally leaden as my hopes.

"I'll have the stuff sent on to your house," he says, referring to the pile that still sits on his poodle rugs.

"Anytime," says Mr. N. wondering if maybe he could discreetly ask for a couple more cans of Alpo or Friskies Buffet without raising suspicion.

"I'd like to make a few suggestions if I may," says Bernie as we stand in front of the restaurant, the warm glow of dinner making us impervious to the cold drizzle. And as we go into a last minute huddle, busily discussing the future directions of *Hearts and Hymens,* I can't help but notice out of the corner of my eye a mumbling, old, hunch-backed woman draped in rags, working her way down the block toward us, trying in vain to hit passerby after passerby for some handout.

"Try to get the pages to my secretary as fast as you bla bla bla," Bernie is explaining intently as I continue to peek at the beggar—the woman so unutterably ragged and smelly, issuing such clouds of poisonous effluvia that people,

149

stunned by the gas, are skirting her in horror. And though the sidewalks are packed with lunchtime crowds, this woman is walking down the street surrounded by a veritable island of emptiness, her filthy, cancerous hands lamely outstretched as she mumbles nonsense into the air.

". . . And I'll have the girl retype them and resubmit them to you for .. . ." says Bernie as the old woman slowly comes our way, shuffling up to us in gaping shoes through which I can count nearly all her toes. And then she pauses, looking for a moment beseechingly at Mr. K.—Bernie gazing up at the sky as though the most fascinating of heavenly phenomena were transpiring in those soot-lined layers of atmosphere.

"I have to head back now," he says, checking his watch, his eyes adeptly avoiding notice of her as she now shifts the weight of her stare upon me.

"And thanks again for lunch." Bernie pats me on the shoulder and disappears into the crowd, leaving me standing with the woman who, having given up, slowly turns away and starts shuffling again down the street, palms up and mumbling gibberish.

"Hey. Lady. Wait!" I call, dashing down the street after her, her slow advance an easy overtake.

"I'm sorry. You almost got away. I wasn't thinking. I've had so much on my mind these days, you couldn't guess. Hey, look, take this," says I, digging into my pockets and rounding up all those stray coins, "I've no use for them. Every time I count them I keep getting a different figure. Nothing but trouble. Let me tell you," I laugh, dumping them into her filthy hands the color of soot and turning away before she can speak; a baffled and dazed look growing on her furrowed face. Need money? You kidding, Bernie? What I need is peace. That's what I need.

A fool and his last fifty-three cents may soon be parted, but nonetheless I feel freed and mildly exhilarated. I was right. Money is nothing but trouble. Better to be flat broke than gropingly poor. A little is far more dangerous than none. The periods in my life marked by true stinginess can be directly correlated to the size of my bank account, the relationship given by the quadratic equation:

$$S = C_1B^2 + C_2B$$

where B is the value of the bank account expressed in U.S. dollars; C_1 and C_2 appropriate constants; and S is stinginess measured in I.U.F.'s (international units of frugality).

Why, give a man a little gold and he turns greedy. Remove all hope and he can afford generosity—fifty-three cents' worth to be exact. Who needs it, I ask you? Money is *crap*. I take a leap into the air. No doubt about it, I feel distinctly lighter, a bit buoyant. A little dizzy too. Is it the wine or knowing that I will have to return home to Viveca minus our little stake, minus a week's grocery money, minus Bernie's pro-rated advance? Money is crap. There, I'll say it again.

It begins to rain grey drops of icy drizzle before I suddenly realize that I have been pacing up and down the same block for almost a half-hour, trying to talk myself out of my predicament. What now? I know I ought to make a bee-line for Uptown and hitch back to Goobersville, but it's late, darkness but a half hitch away; besides, I can't quite bear to face Viveca. Not that she will reproach me. It's her damned stoical Scandinavian silence that'll get me. I knew I

152

should have listened to my mother and married some loud-mouthed, semitic bitch who would know how to exorcise my gnawing guilt.

The ice rain picks up. People begin charging up and down the street. Men and women rushing along the wet, slushy pavement with *purpose*. Businessmen in trenchcoats taking long wide strides, attaché cases swinging in unison from their arms, office girls in fur-trimmed coats trotting on super-high platform shoes, clippety-clop-clippety-clop, leaving behind them trails of perfume that smell of heat and sex and sin and Woolworth and bus exhaust. *Purpose.* Oh, how I love that word. I will put it down on my list together with *fun* and *success.* All worthwhile goals. And what do you know, another winner! *Goals.*

Quickly I scribble down those gems, etch them indelibly on my addled brain adjacent to that area reserved for all those wonderful, though yet to be written, classics. Money? It's crap, let me tell you. Poison.

Poison? And assaulted by a spear of memory I suddenly recall seeing my father pounding this very same street dressed in his bow-tie and baggy pants suit, Daddy filled with *purpose,* out to hustle orders, his dignified appearance belying that desperate frenzy gnawing from within. Fear. About what? About money, what else? Daddy, so worried he was, he began taking orders in his sleep—the poor man ultimately consuming himself, the poison coursing through his veins, the old man whipped and whipping himself until his arteries hardened to stone and his blood burst out the roof of his brain.

But there's a difference. History doesn't have to repeat itself. As Trotsky said, "The first time is tragedy, the second time, farce." And I'll be damned if I'm going to perpetuate this farce!

Money. Shit. I can't get it off my mind. If I hadn't given the old beggar fifty-three cents, I'd at least have car fare uptown, maybe enough to make a few calls. See. There's that old poison. But look on the bright side, Nudelman, you mumbling idiot, things aren't really half bad. At least now you've got both a *purpose* and a *goal*. And at such a bargain. Money. It's got the whole globe hungrily scheming for its venom, gulping it down as if it were the elixir of youth, trying to cash in on all that deferred pleasure. Even in bucolic little Goobersville they are plotting—Ph.D. dropouts like Arthur Holt, forsaking the study of music composition to schlag some new-fangled Japanese hifi gear. Who can get rich studying notes? Or Nyeri, my little African friend, that maniac with his get-rich-quick schemes, trying to re-invent the zipper or develop an electronic mousetrap utilizing a laser. "All you have to do," says Nyeri, his eyes sparkling, "is have something that everybody wants." Yes. To the point. Precisely! Nyeri, you're a regular genius. And what does everybody want? You said it, a little of the old strychnine coursing through their blood and turning their veins to granite, popping their eyes and forcing the blood out the roofs of their brains like the spout of a whale. Yes, plotting and manipulating. Like the McPhersons, both pulling in juicy salaries, yet trying to supplement their poison by selling "personalized sexual fantasies" through the skin mags—just include your name and that of your partner and three dollars in pure arsenic, no stamps or checks, please. We'll handle the rest, thank you.

The rain stops. Damn, what am I going to do? All I need is a little gold, enough to poison me back to G-ville, a little dose of green cyanide to tide me over until I endorse my disability checks . . . Maybe I should go back up to Bernie and lay it on the line. Tell him how I'm just too exhausted to hitch back home, how I'd sell my soul for a bus ride back or a warm bed. No! I'd rather be dead. Never. Do I need money? You kiddin'?

The streets have thinned. People are back in their little burrows busily sending out letters, memos, telegrams, contracts, statements, orders, bills, and checks; achieving in one fell swoop fun, success, goals and above all having *purpose*. So who do I call for compassion? Maybe I should try to find that lady beggar and ask to borrow enough for a subway token. Naah, she'd probably deny that I ever gave her the money. Who can I ask again for that helping hand? Show me the hand that I have not nibbled and gnarled to the bone and I will lick it in rapture. Maybe somewhere in this rapacious city there's some kind, rich, old lady who would like to be a patron of the arts—some genial dowager who has nothing to do with her money and needs a *purpose*. Oh, for a woman like that I would write like an angel. So maybe she's got some quirks. Maybe she likes to see nude men. So I'll dance naked on her dresser, stand on my hands and do a split, dangling aloft my fandoodles while uttering obscenities—if that's what turns on old ladies. Anything for—Wait! Obscenities. Yes. There is someone in this city I can still call. Leo. But of course! Why didn't I think of him earlier? It's as though I'm only able to think creatively under pressure. Now, if anybody's a soft touch, it's got to be Leo whom I've known ever since those first miserable Brooklyn Poly days. A diligent fellow bridgewalker he was, until he dropped out and deserted me for greener concrete. Though, if it hadn't been for me, he would never have made it through his first and only two semesters of Electrical Engineering—Leo keeping mc up until two in the morning in those last ditch, last minute phone tutorials in Electromagnetic Fields, not to mention a year's worth of fraudulent physics lab reports I had to concoct because Leo, my flighty lab partner, was too busy living life to sit in those airless cells like all us other ball-less drones. I've got to hand it to Leo. Even if he didn't have the slightest inclination for mathematics, he was sharp enough to leave and leave early—if only to become an English major. Me it was to take another seven years of grinding away like an idiot before I finally awoke. Strange, that after all those years we were to meet in the same bleak backyard of word mongers—

155

though Leo is certainly better off in the money department (if he hasn't been fired yet), laboring each day as a dedicated writing teacher for the creatively illiterate of Brooklyn, imparting to his gaping students the inside dope on just how one becomes the successful writer he'd love to be.

My mind, fired by renewed hope, begins to heat up with activity. All those calculus solutions and lab reports must be worth *something*. And even if I did borrow a little against the accounts last spring, surely there must be some outstanding balance—say, for a rough figure, twenty dollars? Hell, Leo's so taken up with the state of his stomach and penis he's probably long forgotten that last measly loan. I know I have. Anyway, a person with regular income has a moral and spiritual obligation to share with those in more trying circumstances. Of course, if that tactic doesn't work—though I can't see why it shouldn't—I can always inject the element of fear into him, suggest how circumstances have a very funny way of reversing themselves, how next year it could easily be *he*, jobless and hungry, who will come to *me* for a little poison. And I never forget a friend.

Why am I getting so worked up? It'll be a breeze. No begging. No pleading. I'll call up and say that I just happened to be in the neighborhood. Just like that.

"Just because you owe me money, and a substantial amount at that, is that any reason to avoid a friend?"

"Money?" says I into a borrowed phone. "Oh. That!"

"Don't worry about it. You can pay me later. Listen, I've got lots to tell you. Where are you?"

"Not far away," I stretch the truth.

"Well shoot right over. The girls and I are getting ready to go to a fancy party—in my honor."

"The *girls?*"

"A little change in living arrangements. Hey, did you happen to bring any formal clothes with you?"

.   .   .

Did I bring any formal clothes with me? I mutter, scooting under a turnstile, imbedding myself in the early rush hour jam. Of course I did, Leo, I think, wedging myself into a D train for the long haul to Brighton Beach. Unfortunately, I left them all back in the hotel.

The doors try to close, catch on my shoulder, open again as I press my pelvis against a fat ass attached to an unidentified body. On the next try the doors slide shut with a little bang and the train strains and lurches, compacting meat against meat, the air in the car turning thick with the smell of wet clothes and sweat and stale perfume.

Bicketybangbicketybang. Rumbling off down the tunnel, the train begins to rock and sway and, turning toward the little door window, I stare out into the darkness of whizzing lights, trying to pretend that I am alone, pretend that behind me there is not that great slice of humanity, scores of people with their own little desires and worries and fears, human

157

beings packed ass to belly, Puerto Rican to White to Black, like so much rainbow sherbet.

Bicketybangbicketybang, sings this great steel human integrator as it blindly flies through the dark catacombs of New York. I close my eyes, rest my head against the door and let the thundering metal pound me into senselessness. Bicketybangbicketybang is the melody that reaches my brain; same killer subway Daddy used to ride, it occurs to me, though I try to push away the thought. For all we know, this may even be the very car he collapsed in, sinking slowly to the floor, unnoticed, until the next stop where he was blindly trampled, the final blows administered by an army of exhausted peers. Subways! There should be a law requiring all my old colleagues to undergo a mandatory year of subway riding—those lazy bastards who were always whining about how hard they worked, teaching a monumental nine hours a week and faking the rest. Stick them on the subways, I say, and let them hang from a strap until their backs ache, their arches fall and they have inhaled the foul breath of a thousand other bone-weary souls. Oh damn, why am I so bitter? Why begrudge them their cushy life of regular checks and rich meals and new cars? If only they wouldn't be so sanctimonious, could be a wee bit humble and appreciative in a world where I have witnessed grown men fight and weep over less than a crust of bread. Somehow it's obscene—I mean the way they mouth such high-minded platitudes, then go home and stuff themselves until they're overweight and sick. And even if they do die a couple of years earlier from cholesterol or a sclerotic liver, somehow it doesn't even the score. Score? What score? Who the fuck am I to keep score?

The train stops and starts, spews out a small mob, gulps in another, jerks and brakes and speeds up. An airless eternity later, it finally leaves the tunnels and climbs up over the darkening streets of Brooklyn, rattling along the miles of rooftops, past curtained windows and crisscrossing lines of frozen clothes. Then we are in Brighton Beach and I am belched out of the train, jostled by a crowd of harried escapees as I dawdle along the dim platform, stumble along a little bewildered as though poisoned and drugged. I'll get some money from Leo and then get out of town as fast as I can, I vow. Tonight.

In the streets, I find that it is already night. The festering skies have started to ooze again. This time it is coming down in pus-like slush. My shoes, not having had a chance to dry since Goobersville, squish loudly as I mush down the street. Along the avenue, everywhere I look, the sidewalks are lined with food stores—bakeries and delicatessens and fruit markets and more, all doing a brisk evening business as though staging this spectacle to rub in my insolvency. And damn, no matter what route I choose, all paths seem to lead past those ubiquitous windows brimming with custard eclairs and sacher tortes, smoked salmons and chickens sizzling in broilers and lines of wursts strung up like Christmas decorations. Funny, I can't remember when it was last—if ever—that I could buy whatever I fancied. No doubt this is a great place for the likes of Leo, all three hundred pounds of him, but for me this place would be sheer agony. I would either have to turn to pilfering or suicide. Goobersville, bleak and cruddy as it can be, is for the better after all.

Soon I am past the stores, walking the narrow streets lined with old brick tenements, the buildings pressing in against me as though wanting to squeeze the marrow from my bones. Blindly I step into an ankle-deep puddle, curse, shake my foot and press on.

"Aardvark" reads the signal button in the lobby to Leo's apartment. Nervously I push.

"That you, Nudelman?" bounds Leo's happy voice through the entrance speaker. "I just wanna make sure it isn't some depraved sexual killer coming up to cut my cock off for a trophy," says he as I stand there feeling a bit low—

though there's certainly nothing like a few Scheckels to raise the old spirits. Christ, how am I going to broach the subject?

"Or maybe it's Alex-the-ass-fucker come to—"

"Leo! I'm soaked. Give me a break and let me in!" I shout, banging on the box to give him a headache.

When I step out of the elevator the door to Leo's apartment is wide open and there, standing waiting in the doorway, is Leo's beloved Lilly.

"Hi!" says I, trying to sound bright as I give Leo's gum-chewing chick a quick peck—Lilly dressed as usual in her boyfriend's undies, the waist of which comes just under her pointy bare tits, his socks reaching her mid-thighs—a little sickening all, but I certainly haven't come here to admire Lilly's wardrobe.

"Come in. Come in," calls Leo, struggling to close a pair of tux pants around his belly. Inside, the tiny apartment is bustling with strangers in various states of dress—hardly a suitable setting for private financial discussions, I fear.

"Here, have you met Cindy?" says Leo, beaming his white smile and motioning to a nineteen-year-old with miles of legs and the face of a moron—also in panties.

"And this is Walter."

"Hi," smiles Walter, busy wrestling with a cummerbund.

"Walter has just been released from Bellevue," remarks Leo matter-of-factly. "He tried to kill himself . . . Oh, and this is Gail," he points at a girl who has just emerged from the shower, wrapped in a towel. "Don't try to figure out the relationships here," says Leo, lifting his thick dark eyebrows that meet in the middle. "*I* haven't even figured them out. Bleech, it's all so disgusting," he laughs.

"Listen, Leo, I can't stay too long. One of the reasons I came—" I start trying to ease Leo aside toward the bedroom.

"And I'm glad you came. Here, sit down. Jesus, you look harried. It's astounding the difference between the way you

160

look in Goobersville and when you come to the city. There, among the squirrels and trees and grass—whatever those things are—you look so tranquil, at peace," he beams.

"Leo—" I try again.

"And here so—Come, relax. Sit down. You want a drink? You want some food? No wait, before we do anything else, I've got to tell you what's been happening."

"Oh?" says I, feigning interest and getting that sinking feeling, his exuberance only pounding me deeper.

"Nudelman," he beams, "I don't know how to tell you this."

"Try," says I, getting a little impatient.

"I've made it. Arrived. That's what all this festivity's about. Made it, and big!"

"Huh?"

"I just sold my book!"

"Hey, that's great," I say, trying to sound enthusiastic, enthralled, vicariously jubilant, though my weak smile must surely be a dead giveaway.

"Do you want to be sick with envy?"

"Shoot," says I, already long past that point.

"This may make you instantaneously nauseous. Lilly, bring over a bucket for my friend Nudelman. Just try to guess what the advance was?"

"I wouldn't know where to begin . . ." I shrug a little sadly.

"Seven thousand dollars!" crows Leo, jumping up and down as I am seriously beginning to think that maybe Lilly should get that bucket after all.

"That's wonderful. I can't think of anyone more deserving," says I, lying through my teeth, able to name one individual right off the bat, but deciding to butter him up a little. "Which book was it?" I inquire curiously.

"Which book?" he laughs, turning to the others who all smile indulgently. "*The* book. The one I was working on last year. You know, *As The Fat Folds*."

"*As The Fat Folds*," I echo, intoning the title with ludicrous solemnity.

"Seven thousand," utters Leo, drunk with money. "And that's just the advance. The first piddle in the pot, you might say." The publishers, he goes on, are predicting that his unique tale of the three-hundred pound, virgin fat man who agonizingly diets down to two twenty-five is going to take the country by storm—at the very least. There's even talk of making it into a full length feature film. "The publishers are calling it a masterpiece," says Leo dreamily, touched by his own words. "A cross between Malamud and Dostoyevsky. MacIntyre, my editor—a senior editor!—calls me every day to see how I'm feeling. Even the president of the publishing company is dying to meet me. Wants to know if it was really true that I didn't learn how to tie my own shoes until I was fourteen. I'm going to be in *Newsweek* and *Time*, interviewed on television," he chuckles and gloats, going on to paint a glittering future that will be studded with lucrative talk show appearances, honorariums, spinoffs in the form of job offers, book reviews, guest lectureships. And all because of the fat that folds, Leo's minor masterpiece, the one that's a cross between Tolstoy and Mickey Spillane. The girls are already busy looking for fancier digs, maybe a whole brownstone in Brooklyn Heights; they're planning—for all of them—a couple of months' vacation in Mexico or the Caribbean where Leo can gather material for his next major work. He's even thinking of buying a car, nothing fancy, maybe a Chrysler New Yorker, something big enough to hold the harem.

"And tell me, Nudelman, what are you up to?" finally asks this celebrated literary luminary, after sketching out for our hero a future that could turn even the most selfless of creatures into a monster of envy.

"Me? Nothing much, *yet*" says I, purposely trying to sound devious. "Though I've got something cooking. I don't want to say anything until it's in the bag, but . . . err

162

. . ."I give a wink of my eye. "Just be sure to leave me the address of your hotel in the old Carib. Never can tell. Who knows, maybe Viveca and I and the kids will pop down for a little surprise visit."

"Great!"

"Maybe you can come up and see us before you leave. All of you," says I, turning to the others who have been listening. Everyone nods and smiles. "We've got plenty of room."

"Listen," booms Leo a little loudly. "Maybe I can help you a little until your deal pans out . . .?" he says, reaching for his wallet.

"Help me? Oh no, please!" I blush as he opens his leather billfold to reveal a boodle of green.

"Hell, what's a few dollars to—"

"No, I wouldn't even think of it," I gush, as the others politely look away.

"Everybody can use a little money—"

"No, Leo, I told you I'm perfect. I've got plenty."

"Here!" he says, trying to force a few fives on me.

"I don't need it."

"It's not for you. It's for the kids. Last time I was visiting I meant to buy a toy."

"They've got too many toys as is. The place is a mess. Those little brats are spoiled rotten. Let me tell you."

"Are you sure?" says Leo, triple checking as I watch him slowly wiggle those notes back into his wallet.

"Positive," says I, firm as nails, "though thanks for the thought. A couple of months earlier and I would have bla bla bla. But now, well, things are . . ."

"O.K.," says Leo shrugging, tucking his wallet back into the seat pocket of his tux pants. "What a crazy world," he laughs, "These days you can't even give away money."

163

Crazy world. Right you are, Leo old boy, I think, still tramping in circles through the streets near his house. And it's high time to leave. In my quest for gold I have turned over and turned again every stone in this nutty city, each time dropping those boulders on my toes. Moron! Idiot! Though the chance is now certainly lost, I can't help but wonder how much I could have ultimately extracted from Leo. Boy did that tidy little fistfull look good. Why am I such a fool? No, I was right! Dignity has no price! What dignity, you pompous asshole? You have sold and hocked everything else. Tell me, is it dignified to be broke? Is it dignified to steal a subway ride? Here was a veritable gold mine, this hybrid cross between Thomas Mann and Bernie Kaufman, forcing money on you, and what do you—? Hell. Forget it, I jabber, pacing over and over those same slushy streets. Look, what's past is past. Water under the bridge. Spilt milk.

The temperature begins to plummet. I can feel it in my bones, my joints grinding as though lubricated with sand. The still water in the gutters is already crystallizing to a thin shell of murky ice . . . Just about dinner time, says my rumbling central boiler, picking up the scent of cooking victuals, of stewing meats and frying potatoes. Mmmmmmmmmm. Time for folks to pull their bellies up to the old dinner table and stuff their faces . . . I wonder how Viveca will actually take it when she gets the news that I not only didn't get that urgent advance, but also decided to treat

164

Bernie and myself to a little lunchtime splash? . . . Oh, how I wish the earth would open and swallow me whole, leaving not a trace of this emaciated body . . . How are we ever going to make it until the disability starts rolling in? From the instant I'm declared incompetent, I'll bet there's an enormous time lag, what with the bureaucracy and all.

On the icy avenue, the stores are beginning to close. A light snaps off. Another there. A clattering mesh gate is pulled across a storefront and locked with a bang. Behind the counter of a bakery, an old man in white apron is busy wetting his fingers and counting out the day's receipts, shuffling through a two-inch stack of money like it was a deck of cards. Leaning against the pane and staring in at him, I can't help but think how easy it'd be to just walk right in with a conspicuous bulge in my coat pocket and request a loan—not the whole thing; just borrow a little. I could take the old man's address and return it later in an anonymous letter when the government starts moving on my claim. Suddenly the man stops counting. He looks up, turns pale at the sight of me and, quickly stuffing the money back into the register, rushes to lock the front door.

Well, that decides that. Some thief, I laugh at myself, determined to abandon this borough, to head up north to the Bronx where hopefully I can hitch home . . . God am I ever hungry again. It seems the more you give a stomach, the more that greedy bag demands. If I hadn't eaten lunch with Bernie, I think, lumbering up the stairs to the el, my stomach would probably be in numb bliss by now. Instead I have to contend with this growling, yapping, little beast.

Well, Goobersville, here we come, I think, vaulting a turnstile and feigning deafness as the attendant in the token booth tries to summon me back.

Mumbling to myself, I march up and down the platform fighting to keep warm. Soon a train whooshes in and squeals to a stop. Quickly, I hop in. The rush hour is over. Though there are still people aplenty, I can have my pick of

165

seats in the drafty car. I sit down on an empty stretch across the aisle from this snoozing grey-headed man dressed in a striped suit and gaudy red tie.

For the first few stops I busy myself alternately gazing up at the ads and studying this well-fed gent's piggy-like countenance as it snores and wrinkles in dream. Then for a while I, too, close my eyes, try to get a couple of winks. But I'm way too riled up to sleep, my mind buzzing like a hive. I'm wondering if I'm ever going to get a hitch tonight. And if so, what will I do if it drops me off fifty miles out in the darkness of nowhere. This sure isn't weather for a night of tentless camping . . .

I open my eyes again, hum to myself, whistle, fidget, exercise my numb toes as the train burrows through lower Manhattan then slowly worms its way up through the bowels of the central city. When my eyes fall back across the aisle, I see this same well-dressed man still peacefully dozing away. Probably missed his stop, I am vaguely thinking as, unannounced, the train slips into the Bronx . . . The Bronx, I mull, letting my thoughts drift; it was here that I was born . . . not far away . . . Here that I passed the first short, though surely formative, months of my life . . . Here that I was to suck the soured milk of my mother's young breast as bewildered Daddy tried to reason out how it was possible to be a distinguished Herr Doktor one instant, a potential Attorney General, and the next instant just another penniless refugee, a cipher, "a nobody" . . . It was here, too, that he finally got that devastating news from which he was never quite to recover: that his mother and two sisters, my grandmother and aunts, had been machine-gunned in some Polish town square as they tried in vain to catch up with him, mowed down as the local peasantry, the same ones who had so willingly turned them in, gaped on in awe. Polish Peasants. Szorskys. Father, I am thinking as I look up to see this skinny guy with pimply, pale face and long, bony hands plunk himself

166

down smack beside that sleeper across the aisle. Ordinarily it wouldn't attract my attention, but the car is almost empty. Somehow it strikes me as weird that a person would choose to sit right on top of someone else, given the choice of a whole line of vacant seats on either side.

I've just about dismissed the thought, when suddenly I see this gangly creep with a dumb smile on his face, easing his bony fingers toward the old man's back pocket. Flabbergasted, I gape on as this scraggly-haired kid brazenly proceeds to wiggle the man's wallet right out of his pocket, casually stopping to take a peek inside it before, cool as you please, stuffing it into his jacket.

For the longest moment I sit paralyzed in my seat, my heart thumping away, unable to quite grasp what I've witnessed. With maybe twenty people sitting in this well-lit car, this kid has just helped himself to the old man's billfold. I still can't believe it. And then I am wondering if maybe my eyes have been playing tricks on me? Maybe he was just picking up something that he dropped at the back of the seat? Maybe it was *his* wallet? Nobody else seems to have noticed anything funny. Maybe he just—? No! He stole the fucking wallet! And right in front of my eyes, I think, getting irked, my sense of propriety offended. Something has taken place here that transcends the mere theft of money, something that appalls and repels me, something— though I'll be damned if I know quite what it is—that nettles me, compels me to act. But what am I supposed to do? Make a big hullabaloo? . . . It wouldn't help . . . But I can't just sit back and pretend it never happened, I argue as this crook slowly gets up and ambles over to the door near where I'm sitting and stands there grinning down at me.

Maybe the creep's got a knife, I figure, glancing up at his razor-like face. Maybe he's desperate for food or a fix? Maybe he's got a hungry family? Maybe. Maybe. Maybe. But I just can't sit on my hands and let this prick think he can get away with this sort of crap.

Slowly, I get up and move over to where the goof is standing bouncing against the door. "Alright," says I, motioning with my finger to where the wallet is stashed, keeping my eyes peeled and ready to duck at the first sign of any quick movements.

"What's up, man?"

"I saw that."

"Saw what?" he smiles showing a line of rotted teeth and, for a fleeting instant, again I'm thinking maybe he's poor like me.

"I saw you lift his wallet."

"Fuck off, man, willya?" he snarls, his grin turning sour and mean.

"Give it back," demands this voice of outraged justice as the train slows into a stop. "You heard me. Come on!" I sputter, pointing an angry finger.

Nervously checking around him, the kid backs away from me, pressing up against the door as the train stops.

The doors open.

"Let's have it!" I menace.

"Ya wan' it? Here take it!" he says, already out the door, snatching out the bills and chucking the empty skin back at me as he turns and sprints for the exit.

The doors slide shut and I stand there dumbfounded, holding the old man's purse.

The train lurches forward, then begins to trundle down the tracks. Flummoxed, I look over to the old guy who, as though sensing the weight of my stares, begins to sleepily smack his lips, stretch and yawn and open his eyes. And, staring across at yours truly holding his beloved piece of leather, he begins to fumble like crazy in his back pockets.

"My wallet!" he shrieks above the rumble, pointing at our hero before he even has a chance to offer an explanation. "He's stolen my wallet!"

"No. No," says I, holding up my hands and forcing a tame smile that I fear looks like razor-puss's leer.

168

"Someone. Help me," he cries, staggering to his feet and frantically waving his arms, afraid to come too close, probably sure that I have a knife.

"Just one second—" says I, trying to explain this little misunderstanding as he jumps out of my way. "Please!" I hold out the wallet.

"Look," gasps an old lady with bluish-grey hair, "that man just stole his wallet!"

"I was just sleeping a little," the old geezer addresses the car of turning heads.

"Get a cop!" suggests another concerned citizen.

"Will all of you just listen!" I shout, trying to hold on as the train sways and bounces, calling for justice and reason amidst the growing pandemonium. "I *didn't* steal his wallet. I found it! Will you—"

"It's empty," gasps the man, motioning towards the purse that falls open in my hand.

"Took the man's money," I hear people mumbling up and down the lines.

"Stole it!"

"Right out of his pocket!"

"Please. It was the guy who just got off who—"

"I saw him take it!" accuses an old colored lady from the rear of the crowd forming about me.

"She saw him," someone echoes.

"We've got a witness," mumbles someone else in the kangaroo court.

"How'd he do it?" asks a newcomer, joining the group.

"While I was sleeping he just slipped it out. Like this. Then right away I woke up."

The train stops.

"Hold him!" cries the lady with bluish hair, electrifying the air with hysteria.

"He's going to try and run!" comes the suggestion.

"Watch out! The door's opening. Grab him!" warns a voice as I see freedom suddenly spread open before me. And lunging for the platform, I feel hands grope out and fasten onto my clothes.

"I didn't do it!" I shout, feeling the mob's tentacles pull tighter as I wriggle and squirm and flail to free myself, the crowd spilling out after me onto the platform. "There's been a terrible mistake—" I object as I rip myself loose, breaking free for the escalator and bolting up the moving stairs two at a time.

"Stop! Thief! Hold him!" I hear as I trip over a loose pants leg and fall flat on my face, crushing my nose and banging my teeth.

"Help! Police!"

"Thief!"

Back on my feet, I am scampering up those last shrinking stairs when from behind me comes the urgent hoot of the train's whistle summoning help, the air rife with noise and confusion.

Toot. Toot. Toot.

At the top and ready to dash for the exit, I suddenly spot two transit cops beyond the turnstiles rushing my way.

Oh God! It's *me* they're after.

Quickly I move back toward the escalators.

"There he is again!" I hear from below and look down to see scores of fingers cocked and aimed at me.

Toot. Toot. Toot.

Trapped and confused, I press up against the down escalator, glance a second time down at the mob, then back up again at the closing cops. And while I'm still trying to figure out what to do, a decision is suddenly forced upon me—a loose ribbon of pants leg rudely jerking me down as it snags in the moving stairs. Fighting to yank free, I see the machine hungrily gobble up the bottom of my pants, taking more and more, the contraption beginning to drag me helplessly down the length of its conveying band . . . Down. Down. Down to the waiting mob I am

170

transported, still clutching that billfold, the machine never once loosening its grip.

"Hey! He's coming back!"

"Where?"

"There!"

"Get the conductor!"

Toot. Toot. Toot.

．　　．　　．

Report #3 From The Group *(as excerpted from a paper presented before the 4th Annual Congress of Pathological Behaviorists in Atlantic City, New Jersey and published in The* American Journal of Aberrant Behavior and Pathological Craniology, *Vol. LVII, pgs. 2335-63, February '78.)*

General Discussion: *According to testimony elicited from the subject and subsequent reports corroborating those statements, Mr. Nudelman, following a wild melee in a subway station which ended in his apprehension by transit authorities with the assistance of nearby passengers, found himself incarcerated in a Bronx detention cell. Initially charged with an all-encompassing variety of misdemeanor and felony offenses (third degree robbery, criminal possession of stolen property, disorderly conduct, vagrancy, loitering and resisting arrest), Mr. Nudelman, according to the same sources, became the object of an intense effort to determine the degree of his culpability in a string of, as yet unsolved, armed robberies recently perpetrated within the New York City subway system by a young man remarkably fitting his description.*

Caught red-handed, still holding the evidence of one of the crimes in question (an imitation leather wallet, the property of one Albert Mulks of Sedgwick Ave., the Bronx), our subject, even in police custody, was to continue vehemently protesting his arrest, insisting in the face of hard evidence upon his highly improbable innocence, vainly

172

demanding justice from a system that functions solely on facts not fabrication.

The purpose of this paper, however, is not to concern itself with the tribulations undergone by the subject at the hands of the authorities, but rather to examine Mr. N.'s apparently puzzling and irrational actions leading, ultimately, to his arrest.

Before advancing the primary hypothesis of this presentation, there are certain fundamental questions which must be considered. How paradoxical it struck us that, only minutes before Mr. N. was to become witness to a pickpocket theft, this outraged moralist was himself pondering the possibilities of a bakery stickup. How apparently odd it is that, instead of raising a furor upon witnessing the theft of a wallet (as later Mr. Mulks was so appropriately to do), the subject decided to 'discreetly' approach the alleged thief to engage in some sort of ethical persuasion. Then too, how foolish it seems that our fleeing subject not only impeded his own escape by tripping over a loose pants leg, but also, by then certainly aware of its existence, accidentally brought himself dangerously near the running belt of an escalator. And finally, how is it possible for Mr. N. to be so utterly careless as to hang on to that incriminating billfold, that sole hard piece of evidence, right up until his apprehension, when the police were ultimately to wrench it from his frenzied hands?

Carelessness? Misjudgements? Extenuating circumstances? Irrational behavior? Paradoxical responses? Perhaps, upon superficial examination, these explanations might be deemed sufficient. However, on the basis of this Group's long history of observations, it is postulated that a more accurate description of the subject's apparently erratic behavior is that, by his very actions, he was actively seeking out further misery and punishment—a deep-seated masochism which demands punishment for his sins and failures, both real and imagined.

174

It is the contention of this Group—an admittedly radical contention—that all *of Mr. N.'s preceding actions, however remote from the final events under scrutiny, are part of a grand masterplan aimed at a sole and ultimate goal: self-destruction. It is this underlying pathogenic motivation with its ofttimes near-genius-like orchestration of events, this subtle contrivance of psychic suicide that this Group will attempt to elucidate in this paper presented today before this distinguished body.*

Hypotheses: *That subject Nudelman was to find himself in a subway somewhere in the upper Bronx, witness to an unfolding robbery, that he was to be injured by a moving escalator, attacked by an angered mob and subsequently arrested for a whole host of criminal violations, comes about not by any unfortunate fortuity, but that this final, and near fatal, disposition is the logical outcome of a general strategy often found well-subterfuged in the self-destructive, self-deceptive and asocial personality. This pattern is a precise pathological progression in which step A is undertaken by the afflicted, fully cognizant that it will lead to X, Y, and ultimately to the desired position Z (see psychograph, appendix fig. A.)—a mathematical background certainly being no handicap in this complex game of life and death, a game in which said subject has demonstrated an unswerving determination to undergo the most extreme anguish and torment solely to avoid a badly needed session with his Group.*

Experimental Observations: *The preceding hypothesis is predicated upon the following assumptions: that when Mr. N. seized the check from Mr. Bernard Kaufman at that fateful luncheon, Nudelman already knew with remarkable certainty that later that evening he would be injured and arrested in a Bronx subway station. Furthermore, this Group believes that the act of demanding to pay for that extravagant businessman's luncheon was hardly the initial*

175

step A of the masterplan, but rather a far more advanced stage, say step F or G.

To be more specific, it is the fundamental conviction of this research body that as early as the day the subject first accepted the job of rewriting the Kaufman manuscript, he was already counting on not only being arrested but, in fact, on being shot and killed by Bronx transit police as he tried one final time to elude his captors in blue.

The supposition that the self-destructive individual can lay such an intricate web for his own undoing is understandably hard to accept, but the systematic observations of this Group, coupled with statistical analyses performed on previous segments of subject N's outwardly aberrant behavior (see regression curves 2, 3, and 6 in appendix B), seem to support (p. > .87) just such a hypothesis.

Hereafter referred to as Bronxian Motivation (B.M.), the pattern proceeds along methodically charted pathways which may be visualized by employing flow diagrams familiar to researchers in the areas of Decision Making Theory and Computer Science. Although the specific breakdown and labelling of steps may be viewed as arbitrary, most B.M. types of cases will employ a surprisingly similar loop-like pattern.

In our model, the decision units and the general strategy employed are as follows:

a) Mr. N. accepts a writing job which he outwardly maintains he can never fulfill.

b) Since he can't meet the requirements (or deludes himself into believing this) he begins to change the entire character of the literary work. In this particular case, he takes a serious work and turns it into farce. Although on the surface it appears that he is already destruction-bound, subconsciously he is aware that the new rewrite will be received most favorably by the publishing industry.

c) The subject then returns to the apparent source of his error—in this case to Mr. Kaufman—where he intends to

176

plead for a second chance, though fully aware that, in fact, he is to be surprised *with lavish praise.*

d) As a result of the spectacular success of his efforts, a celebration ensues—in this instance the subject and his alleged employer go for lunch.

e) Thus follows the refractory stage wherein the subject sets himself on a direct collision course. In our model it is accomplished by N. seizing the check and stubbornly insisting upon paying the full amount, including in such payment as substantial a gratuity as will pass unnoticed.

f) (optional extra step) Disappointed that his machinations have not proceeded strictly to plan (i.e., subject N. has not been quite able to do away with the last of his very limited funds) the patient may often employ a suitable "patsy" as a corrective step (here Mr. N. uses a beggar, though some subjects have been known to go so far as to utilize garbage cans or even pretend that they have lost money which is still in their pockets).

g) At this juncture in the game, the stage is finally set, the calamity imminent, solely a question of timing. The division of the remaining sub-steps is now purely arbitrary. We have decided to employ seven units primarily because seven is a lucky number.

    i) Out of money, Nudelman now has an excuse to waste *time.*

    ii) He goes to friend Leo's house, ostensibly to ask for sorely needed financial assistance.

    iii) Leo generously offers said assistance.

    iv) Nudelman flatly turns down the offer, denying his purpose for the visit.

    v) Now the time is nearing for the execution of N.'s masterplan. Employing the pretext of busily undergoing self-debate—though with a sharp eye on the clock—the subject traipses around the Brighton Beach streets, muttering spurious complaints about being starved, even though he has eaten and eaten well in the last six or seven hours.

177

vi)   Nudelman gets on the subway for the Bronx, purportedly to hitchhike upstate.

vii)   Reaching the Bronx border, the patient suddenly looks up to see the pre-arranged pickpocket who has been waiting for him, a long-awaited rendezvous with a contrived destiny finally consummated. Having returned to the place of his birth, the subject can now degrade, punish, and possibly even kill himself in a classical manifestation of the Wysenkroft Life-Death Loop syndrome (Wysenkroft and Fitch, 1966), the cycle culminating through the use of conveniently baited and morally outraged bystanders recruited to insure that the subject's requirement for punishment will be adequately met.

Note: *The fact that Mr. N. was not shot, but rather tackled by the arresting officers, is solely the result of the officers being under strict orders to limit use of their weapons following a recent series of vociferous neighborhood complaints involving police brutality.*

Conclusions and Prognosis: *It is the unanimous opinion of this investigative body that, given a new chance, subject N. will no doubt acquit himself better next time. Having failed to carry out his own execution, the subject must now initiate the same B.M. type gameplan, starting again at point A by, perhaps, sabotaging the remaining pages of employer Kaufman's manuscript.*

The only conceivable alternative to such dangerously repetitive behavior would require the immediate institutionalization of the subject, during which time he would be forcibly required to attend therapy sessions, meeting with his Group until such time as they feel confident that he has provided them with a complete confession and that his antisocial, amoral, self-deceptive, arrogant, self-righteous, suicidal and smug tendencies have been permanently eradicated.

I think I have now touched bottom, the darkest point in an otherwise merely bleak existence. I have been mugged, slugged, frisked and insulted. They've even taken my belt, these keepers of the peace, taken that and my shoelaces and tossed me into a holding cell—though a lot of good the belt did, having been pulled into the last notch and still not tight enough to hold up my pants. What are they afraid of, anyhow? That I'll thread myself up with my laces? Ha! In my state the act of suicide would be nothing less than an optimistic gesture. Given my luck, chances are pretty good that there really *does* exist a purgatory (devout worshippers like the Szorskys having been right all along). Worse still, maybe purgatory means being recycled again through this. I'm too cowardly to risk that contingency.

Crap! I hiss, disgustedly kicking at the bars. Three times already I've tried calling Leo, but the line is always busy. Probably left the phone off the hook lest his dreams of imminent fame be interrupted. Damn, but I've got to get someone in New York to vouch for me, tell them who I am.

"Hey, guard! Guard!" I rattle the bars loudly, but this time no one comes. I suspect they're a little sick of my traipsing back and forth to the phone—but I still haven't gotten my dime's worth and I know my rights, I do.

In the morning, if I don't come up with a lawyer they're promising me a public defender. Yippee. Do I get Perry Mason or some nearly disbarred alcoholic on the skids? If only I could make some sense out of all this, at least find some rationale that might give this torture purpose . . .

"The best steel must go through the fire," suggests the Chairman, still vying for my attention.

"Adversity shapes character," adds Number One, the aspiring theologian.

"Aw, come off it. Save your wind," says I, shrugging them off. Don't they *ever* sleep?

And to top it all off I'm famished, nothing but skin and bones, look at me. And there's not a morsel to eat until morning. Just my luck to get arrested *after* dinner . . . If a man is really what he thinks about, then I am one long hotdog smothered with all the trimmings. And if a man is what he eats, then I am one big nothing, a zero, a cipher, a nobody. That's me. Armed robber third degree, public enemy number one. What a joke. As Leif would say, "That's so funny I forgot to laugh." . . . Can you imagine this? But damn, the way the law functions in this city I'd say the odds are pretty good for a conviction . . . Shit, I'm as good as convicted. Maybe I should plea-bargain, throw myself on the mercy of the court?

Mercy? This is no laughing matter. This is not your run of the mill petty little crime. This is the big time. A felony. Years up the river. And I know they're out to screw me. Even the description is supposed to fit, you heard it . . . But then again I'm beginning to wonder, maybe I *did* do it—whatever it is . . . Shit, in this business you can't be sure of anything any more.

.   .   .

Midmorning. Where can Bernie, Mr. Kaufman, sir, be? It's been hours already since I succumbed and left word with his answering service. They begin arranging the lineup in front of a steel door, yours truly discreetly placed in the midst of four other men of similar appearance though dubious social background . . .

180

Wait. Wait. Wait. That's all I do. When I get out of this trap I'm going to sue these bastards for false arrest and wasting my valuable time—which is not a bad way of making some money, unless, of course, I get indicted for whatever it is they've got cooking.

Come on, come on, I shuffle impatiently, let's get this circus on the road. And as I stand there waiting for this final nonsense to begin, I'm suddenly wondering if *Goobersville Breakdown* is not at all—as I've been led to believe—about the disintegration of social order or law enforcement or justice, but is rather only a fiendish test designed to probe the endurance limits of the human soul, to determine the precise amount of punishment that can be inflicted upon a human being before he snaps like an overstretched rubberband? Which is certainly an intriguing idea except that if my suspicions are true, then *I* am the guinea pig being prodded and provoked in an attempt to discover *my* limits . . . Where the hell can Bernie be? It shouldn't have taken more than a half hour to come up here . . . though, I have to admit sheepishly, there are extremes to which no one should have to go just to get their novel rewritten, regardless of its contents.

"O.K. Now keep in line," calls the jailer opening the door. "And when you come to the platform I want you to stop in the middle. And no talking unless you're addressed. Got it?"

'Well, here we go,' I think, following like a robot. 'Show time, folks.' And marching in line like a good little convict, I am led into a bare windowless room, darkened except for the flood-lit podium upon which I stand with my other 'friends'. Nervously I squint out into the darkness, see nothing but a few figures milling about in front of what must be a one-way mirror.

"Number three," suddenly calls out a voice, "Step forward."

Pause.

"Number three, you, come on!"

"Who *me?*" asks me, who is number three no matter which way you count the five of us criminals.

"Yeah, *you!*"

Obediently I step forward, knees trembling slightly.

"O.K. I want you to tell us loud and clear what your name is."

Irritated and hungry as ever, I stand tight-lipped at the front of the stage as I sense all eyes upon me.

"Come on," calls the casting director for this, my first and final audition for a part I never wanted. "What's your name?"

Silence.

"Out with it!"

"Talk or we'll help you find your tongue!" menaces a new voice from the darkness.

"Oh. Si. Me nime ees José Jiminez," says I with a twisted smile. "Yo no spekka la lingua de usted, por favor, pero—"

"Cut it out!" snaps the goon in front, who would no doubt love to assist in the search for my tongue, except that there might be witnesses.

"Oy, you mean dis von?" says I going into my Yiddish number, determined to reap a few meager pleasures. "Or does yah wan' dis one, boss?" says I, giving it a little racial overtone.

"O.K., step back number three."

"Oh, no. I'm not stepping back. You wanted me to speak, all right, I'll speak," says I, turning red like a beet, furious sweat streaming down my face. Oh no siree, they're not going to get rid of me that easily. "Now *I* want to ask *you* all a few questions. Like, for instance," I fire, "what about my rights? My civil rights? My human rights?"

"Step back!"

"Sure, I'll step back, but what about my constitutional rights? What about the Miranda decision? Where's my attorney? Where's my belt? How the hell do you expect me to walk around on a stage without a belt? If my pants fall

182

down you'll arrest me for indecent exposure. It's all a frame-up. And I'm clean, see! You want to arrest me with cause, huh? Step up here and I'll give you cause. I want you all to know—every one of you present here today—that you're going to regret this. I'm going to have you all arrested for conspiracy to deprive me of my civil rights. I am going to take suit, not only against the city and police department, but against each one of you *individually*. I'll have your badges and I'll garnishee your wages. I'm going to . . ." babbles number three, as he is lifted off the ground by two bulls and dragged off the line-up back to his cell shouting, "False arrest, conspiracy, and brutality! You're all witnesses. I'm going to subpoena each and every one of . . ."

.   .   .

Hardly have my keepers escorted me back to my cell, managing along the way to impress upon me with a few discreet blows, their utter dislike for malcontents, than I am again quickly hustled out of my cage.

"What's up?" I ask, led to a desk where my worldly goods, taken last night, are spilled out before me.

"The charges've been dropped," says my grey, pinch-faced keeper.

"Dropped?" I question dumbfounded, as I hurriedly hook up my belt and laces. Dropped? Just like that? I marvel, beginning to sense the powerful source of my benefaction.

Sign here, they say and, after scribbling my moniker with lightning speed, I hurry after the guard down the corridors and through the last series of doors.

What now? I am thinking when woops, my heart taking a nervous little hop, who do I spot but good old Bernard Kaufman, businessman and author, standing at the far end

183

of the room lost in thought as he stares down at his polished shoes.

"Bernie!" I beam, rushing over to him as he looks up distractedly at a freed prisoner ready to embrace his emancipator—Mr. K. looking distinctly pale, his face drained and drawn as though suffering the lingering side-effects of shock. And at the sight of disheveled me, this ordinarily slick-spoken tycoon, this master of the English tongue begins to stutter.

"W-w-what h-h-happened?" he stammers, looking me up and down, alarm and bewilderment flashing red and white on his face like a neon sign.

"Look, I'm really sorry I had to call you like this," I apologize, regretting pulling Bernie into the endless mire of my life.

"Did the police do *this* to you?" he asks taking a step backward, either to maintain a safe distance or survey my rags and wounds—hard to say which.

"No, no. In comparison to what I've been through, they were almost pleasant." And it is then, standing there on that cold marble police floor, that I finally spill the beans, tell Bernie of yesterday's tragic sequence of events: how I was beaten and robbed, the hoodlums taking not only my last cent, but my bus ticket as well, how, moments later, wandering the subway in a daze, I was picked up by the police and accused of vagrancy and a host of other concocted charges. "I really don't know how to thank you enough. I tried calling friends here in town, but I couldn't reach a soul. I tried bla bla bla. Even my attorney was somewhere in Haiti on vacation—can you imagine that? In the end you were the only one I could turn to," I gush with all the gratitude I can muster. "I'm awfully sorry having to . . ."

"Yes. Yes," says Bernie a little coldly and I'm not quite sure if either of us really believes the story.

"Don't know how I can ever make this up to you," I smile

taking his hand, pumping it fiercely, then quickly heading for the door.

"But, where are you going?" he calls after a moment's hesitation, Bernie hurrying after me down the stone steps into the chill Bronx air.

"Home," says I rather matter-of-factly, the wind whistling through the rifts in my pants.

"Home? But how are you going to *get* there?"

"Get there?"

"Your bus ticket. I thought it was stolen?"

"Bus—? Oh! Right!" I smile chagrined, dramatically slapping my forehead.

.　　.　　.

In the taxi down to the Port Authority Station Bernie, usually voluble, says not a word, not even about his book, just stares mutely out the window. Is he furious, I wonder? Disgusted? Touched, but afraid of showing his emotion? Indifferent? Christ, Bernie, at least say something?

As we drive through midtown Manhattan, the meter already ticking up a very tidy little sum, Bernie finally turns to me and in a gentle voice inquires, "Have you had any breakfast?"

"No," I fib, the words springing from my lips like a knee-jerk reflex. Anyway, what's a little white lie amidst an ever-growing treasure trove of mendacity? Furthermore—if my reckoning is right—I do think it's Bernie's turn to treat. And if I don't take advantage of it now, who knows when, if *ever*, there'll be another opportunity? If we're going to part company, I speculate, let's at least do it over some grub.

In the mid-fifties, by coincidence not far from where Stephie had dropped me off, Bernie has the cabby pull over. After Bernie forks over a wad of bills via the little drawer in the bulletproof partition, we get out and head to a small joint where, I strongly suspect, Bernie is unknown—Mr. Kaufman still maintaining a discreet distance from me as we cut across the street.

Then we are in that warm, aroma-filled luncheonette where, rotating my bottom on a swivel chair like a restless kid, I grab for the menu. Eagerly I give the waitress my order: a pile of hot cakes with syrup and mounds of melting butter, side order of bacon, orange juice, hot coffee, a fresh prune danish, and a slice of melon. Bernie settles for a cup of coffee. Black, please. And as Bernie delicately sips his coffee, his pinky ring giving off a blinding flash, I begin to devour the nourishment before me, occasionally glancing up at my benefactor with my thankful puppy eyes, appreciatively wagging that imaginary tail of mine. Funny, despite last night's gruesome experience, despite the incarceration, inhuman treatment, degradation, torn clothes and lack of sleep, I feel remarkably chipper—a living testimonial to the healing power of food. But then too, when someone stops hitting you on the head, it's bound to feel better.

"Some more?" inquires nice Bernie as I begin to bubble my thanks anew, offering to lick his beringed hand as though it were the Pope's.

Then, a quick wipe of the chops with a napkin, a short taxi hop downtown and, minutes later, the pair of us are standing in line at the Greyhound ticket counter where Bernie is buying our hero a one-way trip to Goobersville. Ugh, how utterly embarrassing to be treated like a child.

"You really don't have to wait around until the bus leaves," says I reassuringly, still brimming with all that animal obligation and wanting, at the very least, to leave Bernie with the promise of my future dedication to *Hearts and Hymens,* except that it would be a bald-faced lie. "I've taken more than enough of your time," I extend my hand as he looks me straight in the eye for the first time today, just

186

stands there peering into me as though searching for something.

And as Bernie busily probes the back of my retina, looking for whatever it is that he has lost, a funny thought suddenly strikes me: what, just what if *Hearts and Hymens* is *all fiction,* the product of a lively imagination? What if Bernie has never been unfaithful to that wonderful wife of his who is always at home knitting? What if, in fact, he never even had sex with her? The thought of Bernie with that scrubbed Wall Street façade of his being a sort of married virgin, living out all his fantasies on paper, is a wild idea, though certainly not one that can be ruled out in this strange world. I will, of course, ultimately have to find out the truth, I think, staring back into those penetrating brown puddles, get—as Leo might say—all the sordid details, spare myself nothing.

"Be careful," nods Bernie with an inscrutable twist to his first smile of the day, disappearing into the crowd, leaving me to stand there a few discreet minutes before I wander back to the ticket window to redeem my passage . . . Nineteen dollars and thirty-five cents. Not a bad take, I think, folding the bills into my pocket and heading for the subway back to the Bronx . . . Not bad at all . . . Things certainly have a way of finally turning out right.

Back now in Goobersville, I find that in my absence nothing has substantially changed. In short:

The Mandels, poor as ever, are busy scheduling, down to the minutest detail, their combination flight-cruise planned for this spring in the Mediterranean—a wonderful opportunity for Dr. M., newly appointed Chairman of the Intra-University Evaluation Committee, to be "with the family" and relax a bit after a hectic schedule that has hardly afforded him time to pee.

During my brief absence, my mother has called to inform Viveca that, upon further consideration and reconsideration, she has deigned to permit me (if I swear to be scrupulously tidy and crumb-free) to occupy her apartment the *next* time I go to the city.

An enormous goodie-packed carton delivered via express from New York preceded my arrival—Viveca opening the unexpected shipment to discover aerosol cans in sufficient quantity to finish the job of depleting the dwindling supply of atmospheric ozone, as well as a lifetime supply of Fixodent.

The Badinoffs, former friends and colleagues, called to say that they were leaving for their NSF-funded sabbatical on the Pacific Island of Titticacca where they will be undertaking an exciting archeological dig in search of fossils of Tricnician Teliditian, a mesozoic precursor of the modern toad—the Badinoffs hoping to sneak in a little water-skiing and golf during their busy scientific schedule. They would like to invite the Nudelmans to their send-off party, but first want

188

assurances that yours truly will not become drunk and/or abusive during the festivities.

On Thursday, sixteen-year-old Freddy Vandervork of downtown Goobersville allegedly bludgeoned to death his mother, father and eleven-year-old sister after an apparent spat involving the use of the family car. Following the murders, Freddy attempted to burn down the family dwelling containing the three bodies, but was thwarted in the attempt by an alert neighbor who spotted the flames. The house suffered severe smoke and water damage, but the car, in the adjoining garage, was unharmed.

I have come home only to be greeted by a tearful Magnus who, by some unfortunate fluke, has not a solitary toy left to his name. It appears that Leif has been wheeling and dealing again, swapping toys with his younger brother. I would intercede and nullify all these devious transactions, except *this* is what life is all about. And the sooner Magnus wakes up to the hard realities, the better it'll be for him.

Alexander Russell, world renowned Economist and G.U. professor, hung himself today without warning in the basement of his Goobersville Estates home—Dr. Russell apparently upset over the latest turn of the economy.

And finally, though most significantly, Betty Mandel has been in a dither all day, unable to decide whether to serve liver and onions or tongue for dinner. I say tongue. Viveca is in favor of the liver. I suppose we'll just have to sit back and wait for the results to trickle in.

And that, folks, wraps up the latest Goobersvillian news . . . though, admittedly, another interesting tidbit has reached my ears. Yesterday, so one of the neighbor boys down the road informs me, the man in charge of unpaid dog licenses came snooping around. Getting wind of his approach, Georgy took his puppy for a walk up into the field behind the house, dug a hole while the puppy played and then, holding him in the hole with his foot, shot the pup, managing to successfully kill him on the third shot. This Szorskian economy move strikes me as a wonderful way to avoid the three dollar licensing fee. Now all we have to do is convince Maud of the enormous grocery savings achievable by doing away with Georgy.

Funny people, these Szorskys. To think, these were the very same characters I once romanticized, casting them as a bunch of salt-of-the-earth, hard-working, land-loving peasants torn from their farm and packed off like cattle to work in a factory. Ha! Given free choice, the Szorskys would gladly sit in a factory any day, assembling gadgets for hard cash to buy new lawn mowers, dishwashers, stereo tape decks and electric forks. One of these days I'll have to make it a point of setting the record straight on this and many other misrepresentations of which I am guilty.

This morning, while in the process of filling out an application for a charge account at the G-ville Mall, I was suddenly assaulted by yet another super way of making a bundle . . . As a matter of fact, since coming up with my social security brainstorm, my mind—after innumerable years of total fiscal inactivity—has been sprouting new schemes like weeds in a dung pile. Deluged with this veritable cloudburst of schemes, I've got to get these plans down on paper before I forget them—though keeping up with them is like trying to catch a rainstorm in a hat.

Yes. The new gimmick. It's a little wild, granted, but near foolproof. Succinctly stated, it involves kidnapping my own children and holding them for ransom.

I foresee this particular ploy functioning as follows:
1) I kidnap Leif or Magnus or both. 2) Shortly after notifying the authorities, the tearful parent appears before the inevitable news cameras holding in one hand a picture of his almond-eyed beauties and in the other the callous

ransom note. Ten thousand? Twenty? The sky's the limit. Take your pick. 3) Now all I do is sit back. Who, I ask you, could resist helping this grief-stricken, unemployed, near-destitute couple robbed of their children? From coast to coast of this great nation of ours, people will be touched to the depths of their hearts. Every day my rural mailbox will be stuffed with goodwill checks, dollar bills, and even dimes and pennies sent in by kind-hearted little five-year-olds in the Midwest who, in compassion, have smashed their precious piggy banks.

Sheer genius, nicht wahr? And it's not even fraud, I think, because I will have never specifically solicited these funds— people just felt like sending a poor Goobersville family a little money . . . Happens all the time . . . And what are a few dimes to a spoiled Midwestern brat, fattened on corn and pork chops, when they could bring such joy to our undernourished lives?

.   .   .

This afternoon a most notable and significant event occurred in the office of my dentist, Dr. Rudolf Rumsey, D.D.S., that amiable Goobersville fat man with the sparkling dome and Buddha-like belly.

My front tooth, chipped in that Bronx station, had been driving me crazy. Every time I talked and the wind whistled past that jagged fang, I could barely subdue the urge to howl. The choice was to either lapse into muteness or submit to Dr. Rumsey. Sensing that fortune was in my favor I decided to take my chances on an "emergency appointment."

Rubbing his hands with glee, Dr. Rumsey ushered me into his office, saying how tickled he was to see me, wanting to know what I had been up to, how the writing was going, why I hadn't had my teeth checked in four years and what exactly was the nature of the emergency.

"Which question do you want me to answer first?" said I being a bit of a wise guy—something that Dr. R. always appreciates.

"Come here. Sit down. I'm a busy man," the little doctor said as a chair rose up from the floor to greet my rear. "Hmmm," said Rumsey, yanking open my jaws and wiggling that unfortunate piece of ivory.

"That bad?" I asked, already getting a wee bit nervous about the bill, disability payments or not, and debating if maybe I shouldn't poor-tooth it.

"Relax and leave the drilling to us," quipped Dr. R., holding up what was supposed to be a soothing hand and, from that moment on, I figured there was nothing to do but ride with fate as he probed, X-rayed and tested that shattered little nipper.

"And now for the sealed envelope with the name of the winner, if you please," joked Rumsey, accepting the freshly developed X-ray from his nurse. "Teedum," he sang, giving himself a little theatrical fanfare.

"Well?" questioned I, wanting to get the damages fast, not this Miss America pageant.

"For *you*, because you're such a nice guy, a hundred and a quarter—and consider that a bargain for a cap!" he added, already eagerly shuffling the cards.

"One hundred and—!"

"So what'll it be?" he asked, performing a few quick elaborate tricks with the deck, fanning the cards like a pro, flipping them into the air and catching them behind his back with a flourish. "Will it be cash on the barrelhead or a little double-or-nothing-draw? Poker? The page number in the phone book? Come, come, pick your poison," grinned Dr. Rudy, holding out the deck like a temptress, knowing when he's got a greedy patient on the hook. This is the same Rudy Rumsey who once confided into the abyss of my gaping mouth that just as soon as the kids got out of high school, he planned to throw up his Goobersville practice, his office,

192

his home, even his wife if she wasn't game, and head out to Vegas to become a dealer.

"This could be your lucky day," he whispered, pulling his stool conspiratorially close to the patient who sat there like a cashless babe with a bib around his neck, a saliva ejector in his mouth sucking away for dear life.

"Twenty-one, usual rules, and *I* deal first," said I, unhooking the contraption from my mouth and getting down to business.

"Blackjack it is," he nodded, shoving the tools off his instrument tray and pivoting it into position.

And then, while Viveca and the boys, not to mention a waiting room full of patients with swollen jaws, sat squirming their fannies, we began our game using former patients' teeth for chips—the plain ones being fives, the ones with amalgam tens. If you play with Dr. Rudy you've got to keep him juiced up or next time it'll be just the regular old invoice from his nurse.

On the first deal, Dr. R. kept asking me to hit him again and again, until I was sure he was busted and just playing games. So I dealt myself, stood pat at nineteen, and watched in disgust as he turned over his cards to reveal a neat twenty-one. The dentist greedily scooped up twenty dollars in teeth.

By the second hand things looked decidedly worse. He beat me with a measly seventeen, and already I was thinking of tossing in the bib.

One more game, I told myself, and suddenly my luck took a decided turn as I pulled a gorgeous blackjack. Not only that, but on every subsequent hand, without exception, I pulled either blackjack or twenty-one. It was uncanny. Neither of us had ever seen the likes of it. First, Dr. Rudy insisted on shuffling and reshuffling the cards like crazy, then he called a time-out as he went to open a fresh deck of cards. But nothing helped—even rolling up my sleeves, which he touchily demanded. I was possessed of the Midas

193

touch. From deal number three on, all I had to do was lean back against the headrest and watch that cozy little heap of teeth pile up on my side of the tray. A few more games and Dr. Rumsey was uneasily mumbling something about all those other patients outside, but I had already managed to win not only the permanent cap of *my* choice, but had also pulled ahead sixty-five dollars!

Would I perhaps want my winnings in future services, ventured Dr. R., looking very much the sore loser.

"Cash, doctor, cash," I grinned in ecstasy.

"I saw that Viveca needed a filling. And your bigger boy's going to need braces soon."

"Looks like we'll have to play for that some other day," I smiled compassionately, polite though firm, eagerly watching as the dentist dragged himself over to his petty cash box and extracted those glorious sixty-five clams— getting money from Dr. R. being, excuse the pun, like pulling teeth.

Sixty-five dollars—not to mention the price of the cap. I *still* can't get over my good fortune! Now I ask you, how many people can go to their dentist and come out sixty-five dollars richer? Though the money is but a drop in our bottomless barrel, like—as aphoristic Perry might say— getting into a pissing war with a skunk, the event is momentous, significant in that it has got to be the first indication, a portent if you will, that my luck has definitively changed. If you believe in things like that. And I do, I do. That little pile of bills clutched in my sweaty hand said that from this day forth things were to drastically modify. Heaven be praised and Hallelujah! Bless the Lord, the holy trinity, Dr. Rumsey and the Mayor of Goobersville. Bless Uncle Bernie, Dr. Mandel and all my other true and unselfish benefactors. Let us rejoice, for this day I am saved, upwardly mobile and upward bound. At this crucial point in life nothing, absolutely nothing can phase me. Let Georgy Szorsky go out into the field, dig a deep hole and shoot his

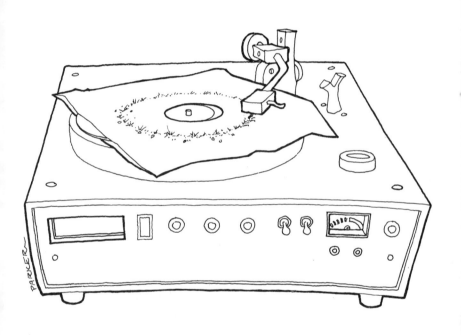

sister clean through the head on the eighteenth try and I wouldn't bat an eyelash. Let him stand on his head and bugger every still-innocent calf in the barn and I wouldn't say boo. Let Goobersville be struck by swarms of locusts and multiple tornadoes, bubonic plague and earthquakes, and I will twiddle my thumbs and laugh. For when, after years of wandering this economic desert threatened by wolves and jackals, collection agents and loan sharks and shyster lawyers, when a man on the skids has finally bottomed out and can only go one way and that way is up, why then nothing, absolutely nothing in this world can possibly touch him.

.   .   .

Put a ten dollar bill into the grimy mitt of a toy-starved waif and you become witness to a spectacle of greed and consumerism out-done only by the rapacious American housewife on the prowl for sale-priced hamburger meat. I want this. I want that. Gimme this. Gimme that. Acquisitive reflexes that know no bounds. Already the two brats are yanking off the shelves items well above their ten dollar windfall, driving the sales clerks batty as they tug at boxes double their size, demanding more, more, MORE. And it matters not what they buy, I have discovered, it is the act of purchase, pure and simple, that changing of the green consummated by the ring of a cash register, that gives the kicks. It is the green orgasm of America, an across-the-board experience that transcends race, creed or national origin. Everybody's doing it. It's what keeps the factories running, keeps us all in harness. Try to talk common sense? Thrift? Delayed gratification? Never! Buy now, get fucked later . . . Though it does a father's heart good for once to be able to dish out those orgiastic bucks like a big shot. Why look, even Viveca has gotten a little out of hand, flushed as she wiggles into some of those better G-ville fashions for spring. Amazing how good she looks in new duds; most appealing, makes me want to try and rip off a fast one with her right there in the ladies' dressing room.

And hardly have we done with that first omen, that drop in the bucket sixty-five, than we are on our way up to the Mall to give the boys a lesson in life: one must buy in order to reject. One cannot sidestep consumerism without having first indulged. It'd be like trying to embrace celibacy with a virginal prick.

"A credit card?" asks Viveca a bit flummoxed as I thoughtfully scratch my chin with the edge of that plastic chip trying to decide just where to begin this demonstration. "How did you ever get one?"

"Woman, such questions!"

"How will we pay for it?"

"How. How. How," says I with a twinkle in my eye and a devilish smile on my healing lips.

"What are you up to?"

"Up to? Down to? And I thought the Inquisition was over. You Christians never give up," I laugh, dancing down the aisles and loading up on God-knows-what, well knowing that tomorrow is C. Day, certification day, the day I will join the ranks of the insanely disabled.

Have you, or have you ever had, Hemorrhoids, Hepatitis, Hernia? asks the questionnaire in the Goobersville Mental Health Clinic the next morning. Paralysis, Palsy or Polio? Do I, or does anyone in my family have, or have we ever had Mental Disease, Venereal Disease, or Idiocy?

Ordinarily, this in-depth health survey, this minor preliminary to my certification, would be easy going; however, I'm so nervous, so over-wrought (hardly had a wink last night), that the first time around I manage to confuse the "yes" and "no" columns. After raising an eyebrow, the nurse comes back to me to double-check, convinced that with a history of sclerotic liver, angina, ulcers, pneumonia and prickly heat, I have either checked the wrong boxes or I am a living corpse . . . or . . . or I am crazy. Ha! Bingo! And without even trying. But boy, am I ever jumpy. Let me tell you. Since ordering that new Skyhawk with all the trimmings—high as I was yesterday afternoon—I've been plagued by second thoughts. But I'm in so deep, what with the credit card bills and all, I keep reminding myself, that this thing has just got to work.

So here I sit in this little off-shoot of the County Hospital (that Krankenhaus that used to serve as a T.B. sanitarium before someone got smart and realized that the raw and damp Goobersville air was killing off those poor consumptive patients faster and surer than any city smog) amidst baby blue walls as my file waits on the desk of one "Dr. Fireside." Hmmm, Fireside? I am pondering . . . A

Yid? Sounds like an alias . . . I've got to figure all the angles. Can't leave any room for error. Like last night I was standing in front of the bathroom mirror trying out tics. Was I going to let my arms flap like wings or permit my neurosis to manifest itself in something subtle, like an ear-jerk or nose-pull? A little wink of my left eye or an unexpected whistle in mid-sentence? The possibilities seemed limitless, the stakes frighteningly high. Above all, I reminded myself, far more important than any tic, I had to be inconsistent. Very important. Also, let the mind drift. Babble jibberish. In other words, *be yourself.* I've also developed a goofy laugh. It's perfect. Once I start, it's so self-infectious that I can't stop. Oh Christ, this is almost going to be fun. Almost. Shit, I'm so tense that my knees are shaking. Good. Knee tremors, add that to your diagnosis, Dr. Fireside. Which makes me realize that I just missed a beautiful chance. What if I had written down on that medical history anthrax or hoof-and-mouth disease where it said "other"?

Stop it! Don't be such a comedian. Play it straight. Remember you're in anguish, pain and debt.

"Mr. Nudelman?" calls a heavy set man, coming out into the waiting room with a file in his hand and, looking at him, I nearly faint. "I'm Dr. Fireside," he says, extending his hand. And as I rise, gripping that smooth skin, I suddenly feel all my plans rush out of my head like diarrhea—for as I live and breath, though I am positive I've never set eyes on "Dr. Fireside" before this very day, have never so much as seen his picture in a newspaper or magazine, this guy is the Chairman of my Group! Or at the very least a perfect double!

"Are you O.K.?" asks Dr. Fireside, seeing me turn what must be grey in the face.

"Yes, fine," I mumble woodenly, catching myself and following him into his panelled office.

"Would you like to sit down?" he smiles cordially,

199

motioning toward a big armchair as he sinks down on an opposite number.

"Why are you staring at me like that?" he asks with a knowing smile.

"Am I?" I laugh, deciding not to be taken off guard if he really *is* the Chairman. God, this is enough to make you superstitious. Maybe I really *am* insane? Screw the mid-sentence whistles and ear pulls. "You look strikingly familiar. Have we—?"

And Dr. Fireside laughs. "Some people think I look like former Attorney General John Mitchell," he chuckles. "Heaven forbid."

"Ha ha. That's it," I laugh my goofy laugh and search his face for some signal, watching and waiting for the pen in his hand to start scribbling, recording these telltale signs of my abnormality.

"What seems to be the problem?"

"The problem? Oh. The problem. Yes," I mutter, pausing for a few pregnant seconds before beginning, my eyes swimming in their sockets almost without effort. "I think I'm losing my mind," says I calmly. "In addition to which I am undergoing a nervous breakdown," I give that goofy laugh and jerk at my ear. "I can't function any longer," says I, a disconnected minute later, hitting on a gem of truth.

"Tell us a little about yourself?" says the Chairman.

"Us?" I stiffen in my chair, almost convinced that I've caught him.

"Merely a habit of speech," he nods, tugging at his own ear. "Please, go on," he urges, his face suddenly taking on this wonderfully soft and seductive countenance as his fuzzy voice lulls away my misgivings and helps me along. Near hypnotized, I relax and begin to tell him about myself . . . about my career as a professor . . . about how I have dropped out of society . . . about how I can't even shave myself in the morning, much less get out of

200

bed . . . about how I am forever confusing fantasy with reality.

"I see," he nods, scribbling down a couple of lines, and then looking up suddenly asks right out of the blue, "What'd you dream about last night?"

"What did I *dream* about?"

"Yes."

"Dream about?" says I, scratching my head and then wiggling my knees for good measure. What *did* I dream about? Hmmm . . . Oh yeah, I remember! "Well, last night I dreamt I was somewhere in Europe on a train. And I meet this luscious French woman who keeps giving me the eye. Most enticing woman I've seen in years. For the longest time we are just sitting across the aisle staring at each other. Then, finally, she lets me know, somehow, that she wants to get it on with me, though she makes it clear that it's *got* to be done standing up between the cars and with chicken livers."

"Chicken livers?"

"Yes. You wanted to know my dream, right? Well, *that's* my dream. Anyway, we're busy frying chicken livers on a little charcoal grill—they do things like that between cars on a French train."

"They do?" asks Dr. F. intrigued.

"In dreams."

"And do you succeed?"

"Yes."

"And how was it?"

"The chicken livers?"

"No, the sex."

"What kind of question is that?" asks I, appearing very paranoically uptight.

"Let me decide that. Please just answer."

"The chicken livers, though, were divine."

"And the sex?"

"Lousy."

201

"Why?"

"I never completed the act. Halfway through I looked down to discover that my penis had turned into a salty pretzel."

"And what happened afterwards?"

"Well then, the next thing I knew, I was having bagels and cream cheese with my dead father."

"Do you always dream about food?" probes Dr. F., now scribbling like mad.

"Yes. That is, when I'm not talking to the dead. Last night was unusual in that I not only had cream cheese and chicken livers, but also a discussion with my father."

"And that's what indicates to you that you're having a breakdown?"

"No! Nothing to do with it. You're the one who started this dream business," I say, getting a little irritated. Is this idiot thick? "It's not the sleep, it's the waking time that's giving me hell."

"O.K. Now let's talk about you."

"Me? What the hell have we been talking about?" says I, getting a little pissed.

"Excuse me. I meant your physical health," remarks Dr. F. quite unphased.

"Oh that," says I, twitching my nose.

"Headaches?"

"You guessed it," I nod, contorting my face in pain.

"Where?"

"Here and here and here," says I, pointing to a hundred different places, all true.

"Constipation or diarrhea?"

"Yes."

"Which one?"

"Both. Depending."

"I see . . . Insomnia?"

"To put it mildly. I get up six or seven times a night just to remake my bed," I admit, invoking God's own truth. "If the sheet's got a wrinkle in it, it's goodbye sleep," I sigh wearily, sensing that this is not going quite as I had hoped, feeling that, for some reason, I have come up against a psychiatric stone wall.

"O.K. Mr. Nudelman," says Dr. Fireside, closing his pad. "Let's get to the point."

"The point? I shrug. "O.K., here's the point. I'm sick. That's the point."

"Yes. So I've noticed. Insomnia. Depression. Delusions of Grandeur. Inability to cope with feelings of guilt. Hallucinations. Frequent periods of catatonia, right? Insufficient feel for reality or the reality of others. Paranoia."

"And that's just the half of it."

"Classic Syndrome."

"Call it what you like," I shrug, getting suspicious.

"I'd call it a case of schizophrenic-paranoic-psychosis with a touch of monomania."

"Fine."

"Though you did omit kleptomania," says he, grinning smugly at me. "Any hydrophobia? Acrophobia? Other aberrations or derangements?"

"Now you're making fun of me!" I snap.

"Sounds to me like you've been doing a little research," he smiles that patronizing smile and then chuckles like my Chairman or John Mitchell—take your pick. "If you had a tenth of the symptoms you claim to have, you'd already be in a straight jacket. I can assure you, you would not be walking the streets."

"So I exaggerated a little."

"A little."

"I do have headaches! I do have hallucinations! I do have severe depressions! I—" I insist, beginning to choke on my own words, salty tears suddenly gushing down my cheeks. "Shit, I come in here begging for a little help and end up getting—"

203

"Please. Sit down," says he, holding out a half-full box of Kleenex. "Tell me what it is you really want?"

"Want? Want? I want *help*!" I cry, breaking down and burying my face in my hands. "I-I can't cope anymore," says I, biting on my knuckles until they taste of blood, hot tears pouring out as I weep for myself, my family, for the misery of the world, for the starving children of Latin America and who knows where else, for the humiliation I suffered at the Gunzs' and in the Bronx, for being forced to "rewrite" a manuscript hardly worth wiping one's ass with, for—for every fucking thing! "I'm exhausted, doctor, *that* is the point. I can't deal with life any longer. Plainly and simply stated, I want to be institutionalized, taken out of the murderous mainstream of society."

"And what do you think that'll accomplish?"

"It'll get the monkey off my back."

"Monkey?"

And then—like a babbling, sniveling idiot, like a helpless and defenseless child—I let down all the barriers and spill the beans, all of them, throw myself on the professional mercy of this doctor of mind and medicine, praying for a minute piece of his heart, for a little human sympathy in the form of his signature on an official document.

"I must have social security or I'll go under, doctor," says I, describing how I have beaten the pavement for going on four years; how I haven't been able to get, much less keep, a decent job; how I sense my family falling apart, falling away from me; how former friends cross the street and avoid me like the pox; how years of living on the fringe of society really can make a man dangerously angry and insane. "Psychosis. Neurosis. Dementia. Call it what you want, doctor, but I beg of you," I say, actually going down on my knees before this man who holds the very power of release in his pen, "Free me. Declare me insane."

"And put you on disability," he laughs, gently but condescendingly, sickeningly paternalistic—that miserably callous fuck of a psychiatrist, that sanctimonious professional who has never missed a meal, never seen his kids go about in rags, never known what it's like to fear the coming of a new day or the long empty darkness of night.

"Listen, Mr. Nudelman," says he, making me despise myself for ever having fallen at his feet, "do you think you're the only one who's got this great idea?" He holds up a pack of files and lets them fall back on his desk. "We see *ten* a day like you. Ten. Social Security. Come, come. Wouldn't we all!" he laughs, ridiculing me. "Look, you're a healthy young man in the prime of life."

"The prime of life," I scoff, "but I can't even—"

"Sure, it's a recession. So you have to dig a little harder. Social Security?" grins the Chairman shaking his head, still unable to stop guffawing. "Tell me, do you think I like sitting in this office, listening to the troubles of every poor soul in Goobersville?"

"You don't like it? I'll take it if it pays."

"You think I wouldn't like an early retirement? Social Security!" he goes on and on, his face red with laughter, and I'm seriously beginning to think that maybe he's the one who belongs in the loonie bin. "What if everybody thought as you do?" asks Dr. F., suddenly becoming sober and trying to employ reason.

"But they don't!"

"Why if everyone *did*," persists this bourgeois, fat-faced doctor of the psyche, this walking social conscience. "Who would there be to drive the busses? To repair cars? To deliver the mail? To run the factories or—?"

"What the fuck has this got to do with *me*?"

"Everything."

"*Nothing*! I didn't come here to get into a philosophical discussion with you about social contracts. I came here for a little lousy human understanding. I. Need. Help. You get it?"

Pause.

205

"I'm sorry," says Dr. F. calming down, his voice growing mellow again, his face taking on these placid emotionless features. "I'm sorry, but I can't help you—at least not the kind of help you want—Look, I can give you some pills," says the doctor, reaching over to his desk for a prescription pad and jotting down some mumbo jumbo. "Here," he says, ripping off the page and holding it out to me. "This is for anti-depressant pills. Try them. They'll help. They may cause some dryness of the mouth, but—"

.　　.　　.

Antidepressant! Now isn't that a joke! I storm out of the wing. Antidepressant? I mumble, trudging back to the dingy Goobersville flats, the omnipresent, chill rains trickling down my neck. What I need is a year's renewable prescription of crisp one-hundred dollar notes, "To be taken before each meal or as needed." That's my antidepressant, Dr. Fireside, Mr. Chairman, your honor!

When the purchase of a single-scoop ice cream cone assumes the proportions of a major family decision, then surely you've hit rock bottom. The "No" strategy, developed in supposedly happier times, has now been carried to the n-th degree. I can't remember when I last allowed myself the luxury of a cup of coffee while in town, much less the extravagance of a bottle of aspirin or tube of toothpaste. Dinner now consists of "vegetable soup," the ingredients gathered late at night from the bins behind the A & P and dumped into one large pot. I don't think I've seen a movie since the premiere of *Snow White and the Seven Dwarfs*. Piggy banks have been raided, forgotten coins rounded up and tallied. In short, we have taken vows of total abstinence from any activity involving the transfer of currency—though it's astounding how nearly everything we partake in as human beings requires the exchange of cabbage. I've even resorted to confining my literary output to scraps of paper, napkins and toilet tissue.

Since that charming interview with Dr. Fireside, I have watched with near-detached fascination as my life crumbles before me, almost every conceivable thing that could go wrong is turning foul in this ongoing soap opera called my life. I have had car troubles, marriage troubles, Szorsky troubles. Even my dog has had serious peeing problems, with the vet urging exploratory surgery at an initial one-hundred-and-fifty-dollar clip.

And on and on goes this mushrooming list that outstrips fiction: there has been a small fire in the kitchen, nothing serious, except that I will need a new ceiling, stove and set of cupboards. The roof developed a minor leak and, checking on the shingles, I managed to put my foot right through the roof before tumbling off the gable, wrenching my ankle and breaking a toe. Everything is going to be all right, though, so the doctor informs me, just as long as I stay off the foot for a couple of months. The waterpump just gave out and we must now haul buckets from a spring a half mile away. Leif was caught shoplifting a candybar, the store manager magnanimously offering not to press charges against the child if I agreed to pay fifteen cents in restitution for the half-nibbled chocolate which could not be returned to the shelves.

And on top of all this, Leo called up this afternoon, collect, to tell me that his book deal fell through.

"But I thought it was all in the bag."

"It was. It was," he said, fighting tears. "All that remained was for the publisher to deliver the contract."

"All?"

"But they changed their minds," he gasped. "Suddenly fat stories are out of vogue. Just like that. Pouf."

And the girls! They're driving him absolutely crazy, he tells me. He's got to get out of Brooklyn or he'll lose his mind—that's why he's coming up next week to stay for a while. The country air will do him good.

And what's *a while?* Bringing only his wardrobe and appetite means that Leo will eat us out of house and home in two days flat—and there's no hiding food from the likes of him. He'll be up here in Goobersville just as soon as he can get his things together. Would I please be so kind as to pick him up at the bus stop?

A few minutes ago, with life rapidly closing in, I decided to call my last benefactor, Mandel, and prevail upon him for a small, additional loan. And do you know what that pragmatic prick comes out with? He says, "If you keep giving someone something for nothing it'll destroy his ego."

208

Ego? What ego? Mandel, you selfish turd with your swollen bank account and splitting stocks, I mutter through clenched teeth, staring out the window to see Georgy and his tractor passing again along the road in front of my house— Georgy having gotten it into his soggy head that the most expeditious and irksome way to gather firewood is to yank out whole trees from the forest in the back and drag the mess home over my soft and vulnerable road. And as I sit witnessing this latest chapter in road wrecking, listening to the moaning of my dog who lies by the door, his bladder the size of an inflated basketball, I can't help but ponder an old but nagging question: Just what exactly is *Goobersville Breakdown* about? Is it the record of a financial breakdown? Nervous or societal breakdown? Breakdown of health, home and family? The breakdown of relations between formerly such good neighbors? Of virtue? Or isn't it, just isn't it, the breakdown of everything that I—this King Midas of human dung—touch?

As bedlam continues to rage and life comes crashing down about my ears, I have come to the conclusion that there is absolutely nothing I can do to stem the tide, nothing but watch and shrug—a strange calm overtaking me as I observe this unravelling comic strip. I am left with only words and, I suspect, precious few of them. And as Georgy happily rakes another century old tree across this ever-scarred land, I go back to the tasks awaiting me at my desk: the tail-end of Bernie's crowning literary achievement as well as those numb scribblings of mine which may one day be *my* book. Both works, it seems, are destined to be tragic dramas with the Kaufman book taking an abrupt and bizarre twist as the protagonist suffers a major blow: Pete Miller, unable to urinate and with a bladder the size of a large honeydew melon, visits a urogenital specialist from whom he learns that he has developed a rare, but malevolent disease of the prostate and associated plumbing—a possibly fatal condition that not only precludes sex, but renders even the most innocent of erotic thoughts or dreams capable of precipitating a landslide deterioration of his health.

.   .   .

According to Dr. Ruben, writing in *Redbook Magazine,* an extra-marital affair depends on what the wife says at the breakfast table before the man goes off to work.

My wife, however, has not been saying anything to me at the breakfast table. Precisely what, I would like to know, does *that* mean?

.   .   .

Another day. A momentous day in the life of this crushed and humble writer. On the verge of retching, I finished the last chapter of Bernie's book. Now all that remains is to wait and hope and watch the *New York Times* Best Seller list.

I awoke this morning as though drugged and since then, have fallen into a maudlin mood. Ever since New York the Group has been demanding that 'complete confession' and last night I gave it to them, all and even more. When they cried "stop," I kept going and when I finished with them, even the nose-picker was holding his ears. Maybe now they'll give me a little peace.

Thumbing today through my old papers, I came across a letter from old friend Arnold, his last before he took his life.

"I am moving along with my painting," wrote Arnold a week before the end, "and try to work at it at least two hours every day. I must literally carve those two hours out of the unyielding rock of daily routines—no small feat in itself.

"My desire to communicate with others has dropped to its lowest point—the need to get involved with other natures seems to hinge on one's power of concentration or lack of those powers . . .

"It is at this point that I must bid you goodbye for today and leave you to Nudelman. The great path of the spirit is there for all who are brave enough to hear its song—otherwise the lower world and demons. Yours, Dr. Monkeynuts."

.   .   .

Life bumbles on. The turds float to the top of the broth. Georgy, having used that fine-tuned receiver of his to ascertain that I am frazzled and on my ass, has been hauling cargo over my road at a stepped-up pace, as though begging for me to flare up and finally murder him.

Viveca and I were up all last night trying to come up with the 'final solution to the S. problem.' Having seen Henry out in the field that evening, chasing after the Szorsky cow with his little stool and bucket, I was struck with the first in a series of brilliant strategies: I will poison the Szorskys, sneak a little arsenic into their meals via the cow, feed that old bovine some mouth-watering corn soaked in arsenic—enough to taint her milk, but not knock her over. Better yet, suggested Viveca, use LSD. Let the cow and the Szorskys go berserk. Which is a super idea, except that it'll probably make Maud even more paranoic than she already is.

Finally, in the predawn hours of morning, I hit upon the best of all possible solutions. I will give Georgy a little 'reality therapy,' a taste of a lifetime's experiences distilled into a few eventful days. It goes like this: First, I will arrange for Georgy to be employed in a lucrative position. Next day I'll have him fired. Then I'll have Georgy seduced by a luscious fourteen-year-old bombshell and then, while

211

he's still intoxicated with his first taste of flesh, get some Mafia thugs to work him over—not kill him, just break a few legs. No sooner is Georgy home with his limbs in casts than our nubile G-ville nymphet will appear with her father to accuse him of statutory rape and inform bewildered Georgy (and his flummoxed mother) that she believes herself to be in the family way. Somewhere amidst the ensuing pandemonium—I haven't quite figured out where—I will prey on Maud's greatest phobia by getting Georgy good and drunk (slip him some rum and tell him it's a new brand of soda pop). And finally, to put the last spike in his heart, I will have sent to the farm in Georgy's name, a lifetime subscription to *Screw Magazine.*

These were the ideas born of a weary mind at four A.M. Today, weather permitting, I will have to check them out in the harsh light of day—though I must admit this most recent one sounds close to brilliant.

.   .   .

On the phone earlier today Leo, commiserating with my Szorsky troubles, also had a suggestion to offer. "You should point your pistol at his head and put a leash around his neck. Make him walk around on all fours and then, finally, fuck him in the mouth before pulling the trigger and blowing out his brains."

I must admit that with the exception of one notable act in his scenario, Leo's suggestion also warrants serious consideration. As we say in the business, we'll have to weigh all the various options at our disposal, no matter how far-fetched.

This morning, amidst further crises, fiascoes and other misfortunes (all too numerous and banal to list), I received the strangest call from Bernie Kaufman—the source of that last enigmatic smile at the bus terminal finally unmasked. Bernie, it turns out, had been sizing me up and now, with a freshly typed manuscript in hand and a contract from a publisher on its way by messenger (the editor raving something about *H&H* establishing an entirely new genre of fiction, a sort of tragicomedy of manners), he had some wonderful news for me: there are more manuscripts where *Hearts and Hymens* came from, in fact, a whole trunk of them. And they're *all* mine. "A job," crowed Bernie, trying to phrase it in language I could understand.

After our brief conversation, I hung up and sat stunned by the phone . . . A job? J.O.B. Work? This time I am cautious, perhaps too cautious. But no more portents for me. No getting sucked in by good omens. No bad luck doing any fancy turnabouts . . . Another ruse, or is it the *real* thing?

"We'd make a great team," said Bernie, hinting that I might well become one of the associates in *Kaufman & Associates.* And he did have a point there. All my life, I've been struggling like an idiot to get my own works in print, yet half-asleep and often drunk, I've brought his work to fruition. Maybe striving for myself I've been trying too hard?

Employment, can it be true? But it *is* true. Bernie wants me to come to New York. He's guaranteeing a weekly salary. He's even got a nice, cushy office already set aside for me—wants me within close reach, said he, where he'd be able to "lend a little artistic guidance."

Yes. A job. Gainful employment. Regular checks. Regular meals. I still can't believe it—though Bernie did promise to send a letter outlining all the details . . . Yes, a position . . . Oh, how I will work to fulfill Mr. Kaufman's trust and faith in me. Unpack your hidden gems, Bernie. Don't be ashamed. Spare me nothing. I am ready to do your bidding, to arrive each morning at the crack of dawn and chain myself to that shiny desk you have made ready. And I will change, Bernie. I will wear a suit, I will rent a comfy little flat for the family somewhere in the Bronx or Queens, buy a briefcase and ride the subway each morning to work. Thanks to you, Mr. K., I will be a person again with title, salary, rank and, above all, *purpose*. I will have *fun*. There will be *action*. I will finally be blessed with *goals* as I punch that clock of yours, Bernie, every hour on the nose, right up until it's two minutes to eternity. And should the earth gape open wide, swallowing buildings whole, I vow to remain at my post, steadfastly honing your literary farts and droppings. Let this country be overtaken by a fresh epidemic of scrofula, syphilis and warts and I will still be yours, Bernie, yours to do with as you want. Only pay me and pay me well!

"Take a job?" asks Viveca, staring at me askance, her face turning white as a sheet. "In New York?"

"Why are you looking at me like that?"

"You'll never last."

"Of course I will."

"You've never lasted before. It'll turn out like all those other 'jobs'."

"I'll make it, I'll make it. I have to. This time is different."

"And what's different?"

"I've matured. I've suffered too much. We've suffered too much. Life is finite. Time is running out. Look, we've had so

214

many years of nothings. I am sick of repeatedly rehearsing what it'd be like finding out that we've struck it rich. The scenario's so tightly scripted there's not even room for improvisation. Viveca, listen to me," I plead as she turns away. "Listen!" I cry, following her. "There are no windfalls. Get that into your head. No inheritances. No lottery winnings. Nothing. And we need MONEY!"

"What's money?" says she in disgust. "Money is crap. Poison."

"Hey, that's *my* line!"

"If you don't have it, you don't spend it. Life is more than dollars and cents."

"Like hell," I smile, a little tickled at how we have suddenly reversed roles.

.　　.　　.

It's now a little over two weeks since Bernie called with his offer of employment. In the interim, while giving the proposition further serious consideration, I've been eagerly awaiting his payment for my rewrite of *Hearts and Hymens.*

This afternoon, as usual, I'm down pacing by the mailbox waiting for the mailman's jeep, convinced that the discreet note I recently sent Mr. Kaufman should bring the expected result today. I sent him the letter a good eight days ago and—counting two days for the mail in each direction, chopping off the weekend as lost and providing a day or so for Bernie's accountant to process the payment—I'm convinced that this afternoon's mail will contain that long-awaited, long-overdue draft.

The mailman's jeep pulls up and, dispensing with even the formality of a quick hello, I intercept his arm as it reaches for my box. Hungrily I wade into my tidy bundle. Most of the mail is familiar stuff. There's the overdue phone bill and disconnect notice. Electric bill with associated warnings. A final notice from a collection agency in Virginia with whom I hold regular phone conversations at odd hours. A new and chilling threat from a firm in Rochester that I've never heard of. But, damn! No envelope to be found bearing that good old *Kaufman & Associates* logo.

Determinedly, I climb back up the hill and decide that, as long as my phone is still operational, I might as well make that long distance call to New York and get this thing straightened out—in a delicate manner, of course. Rehearsing in my head the spiel I will give Bernie about his minor oversight, I dial his number and wait. The phone rings once on the other end, then there's an abrupt pause which is followed by another type of ring. An operator comes on.

"What number are you calling?" she asks.

I give her Bernie's number.

Pause.

"I'm sorry," she says, "but that number has been disconnected."

"What? Are you sure?" I ask and, for safety's sake, I repeat the number and we go through the whole routine again.

"Yes, sir. That number's been disconnected."

Baffled, I hang up and call New York City information.

"I'm looking, sir," says the information operator, "But I see no listing for a *Kaufman & Associates.* Are you sure you're spelling it correctly?"

"Of course. But it was there. In the phone book. I saw it myself in New York a couple of weeks ago," says I, getting very uneasy and beginning to wonder if the Group hasn't been playing tricks on me again.

"Would you like to speak with my supervisor?" asks the information lady.

"Yes. Yes. Please."

There's a long hold and then this other woman comes on. "Sir?"

216

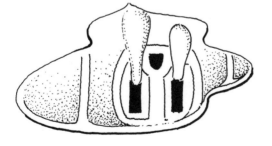

"Yes? Yes?"

"Checking our listings, I notice that there *was* a *Kaufman & Associates* at 475 Madison Avenue. However, that phone has been disconnected at the request of the customer."

"Oh . . . " says I, breathing a little easier, "And they left no forwarding number?"

"None that we know of."

"Maybe it's an unlisted number?" I inquire hopefully.

"Although we wouldn't have the number, we'd know if there was an unlisted number."

"Oh . . . I see." I put down the receiver, decidedly confused. Now what? I think, scratching my head and deciding to straighten out this whole morass by calling Mr. Z.

"Hello, Nudelman," coughs Mr. Z., "What's the matter?"

"There's just something strange going on. I've been trying to call Bernie Kaufman and I just can't seem to get through. His number's been changed or disconnected—"

"You didn't hear?"

"Hear? Hear what?"

"Didn't someone tell you? He died."

"Died?" I gasp.

"Nearly two weeks ago. Of a heart attack. At fifty-four! They found him on the floor of a hotel room in St. Louis."

"St. Louis? But what about my check?" I blurt out.

"He didn't pay you?"

Silence.

"Listen, Nudelman. I've got more bad news for you. He died penniless."

"Penniless? Bernie? Bernie Kaufman?"

"Two days before he died he filed for bankruptcy."

"I- I- I don't understand," I stutter dizzily, my world jerked out from under me. "I mean, he wrote that book, *How I Made A Million*—or whatever it was."

"Look, don't feel so bad," consoles Mr. Z. hoarsely. "He had all of us fooled. Me alone he owes a couple of thousand in commissions. I mean *owed*. He never made a million dollars. That was just a book. He didn't have anything. Nothing. He died a poor man."

"A poor man?" I echo emptily. I hang up and sit by the phone deflated, sit there and stare out at the long icicles dripping from the eaves of my house. Drip-drip-drip they go and by the time I turn back to the silent phone, I suddenly realize that I, too, am crying, huge gobs of tears that roll down my cheeks and splatter in my lap, as it slowly begins to dawn on me what Bernie's last enigmatic smile really meant.

"Neil. For heaven's sake. What's the matter?" asks Viveca.

I look up at her, struggle to speak, try to explain what's happened, but my voice cracks and deserts me. I take a deep breath and try again, but just can't talk. I can't find any words, I suspect, because I simply don't know how to begin or really what to say. I'm not even sure if I'm crying because of Bernie's sudden death in a far off hotel room, because of my eight-hundred-dollar check that I will never receive, because his passing is somehow a painful reminder of my own mortality, or . . . or because of all three. Perhaps I'm weeping because this one thing in life that I had thought was so rock-solid, this Bernie Kaufman with his smooth-skinned, unrippled exterior, his diamond pinky ring and fancy digs, his tailored suits and self-assurance, this Bernie Kaufman that I had come so close to worshipping and looking upon as my savior, was nothing but front, a well-groomed, elaborate but penniless façade . . . Because Bernie Kaufman, for all his apparent insouciance, was living as much on the raw edge of life as I. Because that last smile of his was one of *recognition* and I was such a thick-headed shit not to see it.

219

Later in the afternoon, as the day begins to give way to dusk, Viveca and I are sitting at the kitchen table. I stare into the cup of coffee in front of me that has long since gone cold. Except for the sound of our children playing in their room we sit in silence.

"You know, Neil," says Viveca breaking into my thoughts, "If you had accepted that job—a job which you'd have hated in a week and that would have made life miserable for all the rest of us—if you had accepted it, I swear, I would have left you and gone back to Sweden."

Pause.

A long silence.

"Back to Sweden you say?"

"Yes. There *are* limits. I really would have gone. I mean it."

"Hmmm . . . Sounds like a good idea," I agree, looking up thoughtfully.

"What?" she flushes.

"Yes. Sweden," I say, slowly rising out of my stupor. "Now there's an intriguing thought. Certainly. By all means. We'll all go," I begin to brighten, drifting off dreamily, seeing before me the bobbing masts of ships lined up along the quay on *Strandvägen*. "Yeah, Sweden," I nod, warming to the idea, " . . . sow a little needed trauma into that well-ordered social democracy that they're always crowing about."

"Neil, do you really mean it?" she asks, taken by surprise,

220

calling after me as I wander out the front door, wound up in thought. "Shall we start packing?"

Outside it is getting dark. The sun sneaks down over the lip of my hill and the air tastes damp of rotted leaves and coming spring. For the moment the Szorsky tractor has stopped and the hills are deliciously still. And I hear birds in the trees, spring birds . . . Things have suddenly changed, it occurs to me. For the first time in close to four years, I feel like a man with options. And I do have options. If I want to, I can go back to Sweden and start all over again . . . Or, I can polish and posthumously publish the works of Bernie Kaufman . . . Or, better yet, indulge myself and finish my own *Goobersville Breakdown* . . . On the other hand, I can just continue to sit here in Goobersville and let the seasons drift by, knowing that this time I really did have a say in the matter, that it did not happen by default . . . I could just sit here and sniff the flowers and ponder and write and sometimes do absolutely nothing—but with an essential difference. This time I would let life happen, let it pass gently instead of forcing it, surrender myself to nothingness, to zero. I would await no redemption. Anticipate no windfalls.

Options. Options. They suddenly all sound so intriguing . . . What I need is a little help. A few devil's advocates. Where the hell is the Group when I need them most? I try to summon that aggregation of pompous peckers, but nothing happens. Try again and again and again . . . Have they left forever? Am I cured of whatever it is I am supposed to be cured of?

About the Author

Born and raised in New York City, Robert Lieberman presently lives in hiding in a small Upstate New York town. In addition to a successful novel, "Paradise Rezoned," his short stories have been widely published in this country and also in translation in Sweden where he has resided for prolonged periods. He is presently a Professor of Engineering at Cornell University—though he has also been a Professor of Mathematics, Physics and the Physical Sciences. His long range plans are "to be rich, famous and have *fun*—not necessarily in that order." Mr. Lieberman insists that "Goobersville Breakdown" contains not a shred of biographical material.

About the Illustrator

Tom Parker, another foul-tempered recluse who lives in the rural fringes of New York State, has done striking illustrations for a number of national magazines which he refuses to identify and, hence, provide with free advertisement. Mr. Parker is currently trying to raise funds for a captive breeding project for endangered species of Eastern land turtles.